"So how come bachelor like y

Brian shrugged. "Ha a wild singles scene.

He walked Mari to the door, and she stood on the bottom step. She hated moments like these. To kiss or not to kiss?

She was just about to lean over when he gave her a quick peck on the cheek, turned around and jogged to his car, waving as he drove away.

That's it?

She rolled her eyes, disappointed in herself for wanting more.

Yet she was relieved that nothing more had happened.

Wasn't she?

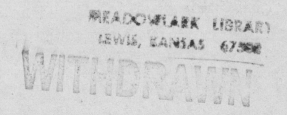

Dear Reader,

Spring is always beautiful at Hawk's Lake, a quaint little village in the Adirondack Mountains of upstate New York. The rivers are flowing and the wildflowers are in bloom.

Marigold Sherwood, an exhausted businesswoman, needs the comfort of the gently lapping lake. Renting her family's grand Victorian cottage from her first love, Brian Hawkins, seemed like a good idea at the time, but she wasn't going to pick up where they'd left off, especially when he'd broken her tender teenage heart.

Brian can't believe that Mari returned to town when she could vacation anywhere in the world. Not only does she still have the power to knock him off his feet, but she has the job he's always wanted. Would he decide to leave quiet Hawk's Lake for the bright lights of Boston, or stay with the woman he's always loved?

So come on over and discover calm, gentle life at Hawk's Lake, and we'll have tea and sugar cookies on the porch that overlooks the cool, clean water.

Best wishes,

Christine Wenger

THE TYCOON'S PERFECT MATCH

CHRISTINE WENGER

SPECIAL EDITION

Published by Silhouette Books

America's Publisher of Contemporary Romance

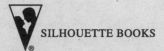 SILHOUETTE BOOKS

Recycling programs
for this product may
not exist in your area.

ISBN-13: 978-0-373-65461-1

THE TYCOON'S PERFECT MATCH

Copyright © 2009 by Christine Wenger

Visit Silhouette Books at www.eHarlequin.com

Printed in U.S.A.

Books by Christine Wenger

Silhouette Special Edition

The Cowboy Way #1662
Not Your Average Cowboy #1788
The Cowboy and the CEO #1846
*It's That Time of Year #1937
*The Tycoon's Perfect Match #1979

*The Hawkins Legacy

CHRISTINE WENGER

has worked in the criminal justice field for more years than she cares to remember. She has a master's degree in probation and parole studies and sociology from Fordham University, but the knowledge gained from such studies certainly has not prepared her for what she loves to do most—write romance! A native central New Yorker, she enjoys watching professional bull riding and rodeo with her favorite cowboy, her husband, Jim.

Chris would love to hear from readers. She can be reached by mail at PO Box 1212, Cicero, NY 13039, or through her Web site at www.christinewenger.com.

To Mary Ann, who has been a great pal
since our SMS days. A sincere thanks for your friendship
throughout the years—through fun times and sad times,
whining and "raspidity." It means a lot to me
that you've always been there.

Chapter One

A shiver of excitement went through Marigold Sherwood as she slowed her van to a crawl. After a six-hour trip from Boston, she was finally driving down Main Street in the little town of Hawk's Lake in the Adirondack mountains.

She soaked in the charm of the huge Victorian houses, with their gingerbread trim, emerald-green lawns and picket fences, and felt a stirring of—dare she say?—happiness.

During this two-month hiatus from her high-pressure job, she wanted—*needed*—to rejuvenate her spirit, relax her body, reinvent herself. Rediscover who Mari Sherwood actually was.

She was hoping that she'd find all those R-words in the place she'd always been happiest: Hawk's Lake, where she'd spent many childhood summers.

Daffodils, hyacinths and tulips waved in the breeze along every spare patch of dirt and lined every path as far as she could see. Bright yellow forsythia bloomed in every yard, and the lilac bushes were budding.

She longed to be out of her rented van and walking in the sunshine. It had been a long time since the frenetic pace of her life had allowed her the time to take a leisurely stroll in the sun or smell the scent of flowers on the breeze.

Stopping at an intersection, she waited for several girls on bicycles to cross and glanced down to check the address on the map that her assistant, Julie, had printed out for her. The real-estate office should be right about…here.

Mari slid into a parking space in front of one of the Victorian houses that lined Main Street. She climbed out of the van and stared at the sign on the lush green lawn that said Brian Hawkins Real Estate. Under his name, in white letters, was CPA, Notary.

Brian was a member of the celebrated Hawkins

family, descendants of the town's founder. They owned the grandest cottage on Hawk's Lake, although she'd dearly loved her own family's summerhouse, Sherwood Lodge.

Every June when school let out, she couldn't wait to return to Hawk's Lake and launch into adventures with Melanie, Jack and Brian Hawkins, and every September she hated to go back home to Boston. But around the seventh grade, it was Brian she couldn't wait to see again. He was the one who could make her heart race and her cheeks heat with just a glance.

And it was Brian who broke her heart when she was sixteen.

She paused to study the cream-colored Victorian in front of her. It had once been the home of Pamela's Perfumery—a fabulous place for a young girl to visit.

As she climbed the stairs, she was immediately drawn to the gazebo-style, rounded corner of the front porch. She stood in the middle of it and could almost taste the lemonade and sugar cookies that Mrs. Newley, the owner of the perfume store, had served whenever she and Melanie, Brian's younger sister, came to visit. They'd sit at a small table and talk for hours, making up stories of adventure and intrigue, sipping their lemonade and pretending they were sophisticated and grown-up.

Mari paused inside the front door and took a deep breath. Maybe it was just her imagination, but she thought she could catch the scent of all the perfumes, sachets and candles lingering in the air.

An elderly woman looked up from her computer screen. "If it isn't little Marigold Sherwood! Welcome back to Hawk's Lake."

"Mrs. Newley? I was just thinking of you!"

"It's been a long time." Mrs. Newley got up from her desk and walked toward her. "Brian told me to expect you today." She embraced Mari in a warm hug.

"It's good to see you again. Just looking at your house brings back so many wonderful memories."

"So, how have you been, Mari? Are you married? Do you have any children?"

Mari's gaze shot to her left hand, where a marquis-cut diamond had once perched. A pang of disappointment settled in her stomach. "I've been fine. And no, I've never married. And no children."

Mrs. Newley shook her head. "What's wrong with those men in Boston?"

The face of Jason Fox, ex-fiancé and corporate climber, flashed before her, and Mari glanced at her bare ring finger again.

Forget him, she reminded herself.

"What happened to your perfume shop?" Mari asked, changing the subject.

"I wanted to travel more—to visit my children and grandchildren—so I sold the house to Brian Hawkins for his real-estate business. When he saw how difficult it was for me to leave the house in which I'd lived my entire life, he suggested that I stay. Guess you could say that I came with the house." She giggled. "Brian Hawkins has a heart of gold. Always did."

Mari remembered when Brian had gone back over his entire paper route, knocking on doors, because he had an extra paper and was afraid that he'd forgotten someone. Or the time when he'd worked as a cashier at Clancy's Grocery Store, and a little boy was short of money for milk. Brian had tossed his own money into the register. Mari doubted that it was the first— or the last—time he'd covered someone who was short.

Yes, Brian had a heart of gold.

Except when it came to *her*.

"So you work for Brian, Mrs. Newley?"

"Part-time."

"Then, would you happen to have the key to my old cottage? And I must have papers to sign, if Julie, my assistant, hasn't already taken care of that."

Just before she was getting ready to leave Sherwood Enterprises for this vacation, Mari must have signed her name thousands of times per day. It was all a blur.

"I can help you with the key, but Brian has your paperwork. He should be here soon." Mrs. Newley looked at the grandfather clock in the corner. "He had a closing at one of the buildings on Main Street."

"I can't believe that it's been twelve years since I've been here. How is Brian?"

"Well, he's still single. If I were only thirty years younger!" She laughed. "I don't know why he never settled down." She went to a desk, slid open a drawer and began searching through little manila envelopes. "It's in here somewhere. I should have gotten it ready, but I've been so busy."

So Brian had never married.

Mari didn't hear much of what Mrs. Newley said after that. She was reminiscing about the pink plastic diary she used to keep—the one in which she'd doodled colorful hearts with the initials *M.S. & B.H.* inside.

As Mari waited, she wondered if she'd even recognize Brian, and if he was still as serious as he'd been when they were kids. If that big Stickley desk behind a wall of windows was his, it was perfectly organized, without a stray piece of paper anywhere. It was the exact opposite of her hideously cluttered office and desk in Boston. But neat, tidy and organized was exactly how she remembered him.

Over the years, she'd often thought about their first kiss during her last summer at Hawk's Lake. She was sixteen, and it had been a glorious June day. They were eating blueberries right off the bush. Brian had been telling her how much he missed his mother, who had died earlier in the year, and they both were reminiscing about her delicious pies. When his voice cracked in sadness, she'd put her arms around him. Then he'd kissed her. It was a soft, tentative kiss at first, then increased in pressure until Brian moved away from her, a shocked expression on his face. The touch of his lips had haunted her dreams ever since.

A door creaked open behind her. "I'm back, Mrs. Newley."

Mari jumped, bumping into the man behind her, knocking a beverage out of his hand.

"Oh, I'm sorry." She pulled a pack of tissues from her purse and squatted down to wipe up the spill from the hardwood floor.

Then she looked up—right into Brian Hawkins's turquoise eyes.

As she rose to her feet, he towered over her and she saw that he was impeccably dressed in a tan suit that hung perfectly from his frame. His tie matched the color of his eyes, and his hair was just as black and thick as it was when they were kids.

There was still something about him—something that made her heart race and butterflies flutter in her stomach. He was studying her with such intensity that she felt her cheeks flush.

One thing was certain—the gawky boy had turned into a very masculine and sexy man.

"Loosen up, Brian," she remembered saying many times as she'd mussed his hair, running off as he chased her. *"Live a little."*

If only she'd taken her own advice.

"Welcome back to Hawk's Lake, Mari." He held out his hand and they shook as if they were business acquaintances instead of old friends. His hand was warm and welcoming, yet she felt herself longing for a hug—just for old-time's sake.

It had nothing to do with a desire to be held in those muscular arms.

"Thanks, Brian. It's been a long time." She couldn't take her eyes off him. "How's your family? Everyone doing well?"

"Pop's retired, but we still can't keep him away

from Hawkins's Garage. Melanie remarried and has a new baby, and her son, Kyle, is almost seven now. Jack builds custom stock cars when he's not racing them himself."

She studied him as he spoke. What happened to the glint of restlessness that had always lurked in his eyes? Granted, a lot of years had passed, but she'd still expected a little of the adventurous Brian she remembered. *That* Brian was ready to take on the world, but now he seemed reserved—or maybe he was just content.

"And what about you? How've you been?" Mari asked.

"I run this real-estate office. I also do the books for just about every establishment in town, and I run the business end of Hawkins's Garage and pitch in and do whatever else I'm needed to do in this village."

His voice turned flat, and his eyes lost some of their sparkle. He didn't seem all that happy.

Playing a hunch, Mari said, "As I recall, you wanted to leave Hawk's Lake and move to New York to work in finance. Didn't you ever move?"

Mari knew that Brian would have needed to relocate if he'd wanted a job that suited his dreams. There was nothing in these mountains other than gift shops, marinas and small lodgings and restaurants for tourists. There were simply no Fortune 500 companies in the Adirondack Preserve.

His smile dimmed, and he stuffed his hands into his pockets. Mari now knew for certain that she'd touched on a sore subject.

"For a while. I spent several years at a brokerage firm on Wall Street, but then I was needed here, so I came home."

"Why didn't you ever go back?"

"And leave all this?" he said, gesturing to the beautiful scenery outside. "Like I said, I was needed here."

Mari could hear the sarcasm in his voice.

"Sounds like you've been busy," she said, trying to redeem herself for whatever she'd said to upset him. "I'll bet you're happy that you came back to this fabulous place."

"Fabulous?" He raised an eyebrow. Before she could try to decipher his meaning, he abruptly turned to Mrs. Newley and held out his hand. "Could I have the keys to Sherwood Lodge, please?"

A warmth washed over her like the sun peeking through the clouds. "You still call it that? That's a nice surprise."

"Mari, you know how it is up here. Everyone

names their camps and cottages in the Adirondacks, and hardly anyone changes them."

"Yes, but I'm still…surprised. It's just that it's been a long time, and—" How could she explain to Brian that it meant a lot to her that the name of the place she would always think of as home—no matter where she lived—hadn't changed?

The cottage would have been her legacy. Just like Sherwood Enterprises was her legacy now.

He'd never understand that it was important to her that the cottage named for her great-great-grandmother, Violet Sherwood, the founder of Sherwood Enterprises, remained the same.

Violet's company had been passed down from generation to generation, and now Mari was the last of the bloodline. After her father retired, if she didn't step up to the CEO position, or if she decided to leave the company completely, her father could promote someone from within, or go outside. But either way, the company that had begun with Violet making pottery in her carriage house would cease to be run by a Sherwood.

She could always sit on the board of directors with her parents and her grandmother, but it just wouldn't be the same.

It was highly unlikely that she'd share her quandary with Brian. She wasn't sure he'd understand how difficult it was to keep a high-pressure, fast-paced job that was sapping her of all her energy and creativity. Sure, he was also involved in his family's business. But he wasn't an only child like she was, nor was he responsible for the fate of a multi-million-dollar company.

"Here you are, Brian." Mrs. Newley handed him a small envelope.

He nodded his thanks and put his hand on Mari's shoulder. "You must be tired after that long ride. Let's get you settled."

His light touch sparked a connection that their conversation had just about extinguished, and Mari tried not to let her awareness of him bother her. After all, they were old friends.

But the weight of what his friendly touch symbolized was more than she could bear. Didn't he remember how he'd broken her heart twelve years ago?

"Do you remember the way to the cottage?" he asked.

"I could find it blindfolded." She moved away from him. "It's really not necessary for you to drive out there with me. You probably have better things to do."

On another occasion, she might like to catch up

with him and to get to know him all over again. Clearly, a lot had changed for them both.

But now wasn't the time to become reacquainted.

"I want to make sure everything's in working order for you," he explained. "The water and heat should be on, and I hired some cleaners. But I prefer to check on things myself. If it's all acceptable to you, you can sign a few more papers, and it'll be all yours for the season."

He was just doing his job, and she probably should let him. She was simply in need of some alone time—time to figure out what she should do about Sherwood Enterprises.

And she had to forget about Jason. What a sucker she'd been to fall for him. To make matters worse, Jason wasn't the first man who'd used her to get ahead. He was the *third* in recent memory.

Well, three strikes and she was out.

What was wrong with her judgment where men were concerned? She was supposed to take the CEO position, but she was the worst judge of character in the world.

One thing she knew for sure. Brian Hawkins could easily distract her from all of her plans. He reminded her of her past—and she needed to think about her future.

She needed to keep her distance from men in general, and Brian Hawkins in particular—a lot of distance. She might be willing to take chances with her career, but she refused to gamble with her heart.

Chapter Two

Brian glanced again at his rearview mirror. If Mari followed him any more closely, she'd be in his trunk. Maybe she didn't quite remember the way after all.

When he first saw her standing in his real-estate office, he couldn't believe how stunning she looked. Her khaki shorts showed off her long, perfect legs. A bright lime T-shirt brought out the green of her eyes and the shimmering gold highlights of her shoulder-length blond hair. Both garments clung in all the right places.

Skinny Marigold Sherwood had sure filled out over the years.

Brian didn't know why that surprised him. He, of all people, knew that time didn't stand still. He often felt like time was running out, and he was only thirty. There were so many things he still wanted to do.

Mari had accomplished what *he'd* always dreamed of—she was next in line to run a Fortune 500 company.

Mari. Her face had always glowed and her eyes were always bright with joy. But now the glow had dimmed and the brightness was almost extinguished.

What had happened to her?

He knew that she was taking an extended vacation from her family's company, but Julie, her administrative assistant, wouldn't say much more than that.

He couldn't imagine ever needing a vacation from such an exciting job. The design, manufacture and distribution of fine china and crystal, silverware, and whatever else Sherwood Enterprises was acquiring or licensing, would be a limitless challenge. It'd be exciting making decisions and taking risks worth millions of dollars.

To be the CEO of Sherwood Enterprises, like Marigold was poised to be, was definitely the job of his dreams.

He knew all this because he'd been following Sherwood Enterprises since he'd first met Tom Sherwood, Mari's father. He was a dynamic person, larger than life, and Brian had loved listening to him talk about his company. Mr. Sherwood would relate something he'd been working on and ask Brian's opinion. Brian remembered how he'd listen intently, and when he gave Mr. Sherwood his feedback, the man would sometimes say, "That's a wonderful idea, young man. You've got a real head for business."

Brian would float on air whenever he heard those words.

When Brian's father had brought up the subject of a high school graduation party, Brian asked him for the money instead. Then he'd bought stock in Sherwood Enterprises and two other companies, expanding his portfolio considerably thoughout the years.

And he thoroughly studied every annual report. Mr. Sherwood's letter to the stockholders never failed to mention Mari. Reading between the lines, Brian gleaned that she'd started low on the ladder and moved up in the company on merit alone, in spite of her heritage. Good for her.

His dream had always been to prove to himself

and everyone else that he could successfully manage a major company. However, his recent conversation with Mari painfully reminded him that he'd fallen way short of his goal.

She'd succeeded and he'd failed.

He turned onto the dirt road that meandered behind the big Victorian-style cottages that graced the south shore of Hawk's Lake. Sherwood Lodge was the grandest of all the Victorians.

He'd had Sherwood Lodge rented, but when he received the call from Julie, he and Mrs. Newley jumped through hoops to relocate the renters to other properties. He could have just told Julie that it was impossible, but even after twelve years without a word from Mari, he sensed the importance of the request.

He pulled into the parking area by the boathouse. Before he could blink, Mari was already out of her van and running to the front of the camp that faced the lake.

He followed her slowly, giving her some time. He heard her laughter and then she let out a happy whoop. When he finally caught up, she was looking at the cottage with a big grin on her face.

That was the Marigold he remembered.

The cottage had several rooflines with bright red shingles. He'd kept it painted in its original colors—

pale blue, with white gingerbread fretwork. The white shutters sported cutouts of sailboats.

He especially liked the stairs, with their blue sandstone caps and the native pink granite walkways that circled the cottage and linked the front and back entrances.

"It's so great to be home," she said, then saw him standing there. She lowered her eyes as if embarrassed, then looked up at him. "I mean, it's great to see the old place again. You've kept it up nicely, Brian. Thank you."

Home?

That was an interesting slip. She hadn't been to Hawk's Lake in over a decade.

"My pleasure." It was worth all the restoration work and the tedious process of relocating several weeks of renters, just to see the happy expression on Mari's face again.

"I'm glad you kept it the same colors."

Was he mistaken, or were tears shimmering in her eyes? "Mari, are you okay?"

She shrugged her shoulders. "Just a little sentimental, I guess."

He cocked his head, looking her up and down. "You could have vacationed anywhere in the world, but you came back here. Why?"

She didn't answer, but the smile left her face.

"I'm sorry." He could have kicked himself for making her lose her smile. "It's none of my business. Let me unload your luggage for you."

"Oh, no," she said. "I'll do it later. But I could use your help in unloading my wheel and my kiln."

"Your *what?*"

"My pottery wheel and firing kiln. The kiln is a portable one, not the huge kind. But I don't want to unload them right now. Maybe in a couple of days." She was smiling again. "I plan on throwing some pots while I'm here."

"Sorry, it's against my rental rules," he said, trying to keep a straight face. He pulled out a form from the folder he was holding. "Here it is, Brian's rental rule number twelve—no throwing pots or dishes. Just after rule number eleven—no nude parties on the beach. Although I'm willing to waive that rule if you insist."

She laughed, and the happy sound echoed across the quiet lake, as it often had when they were kids.

He liked seeing her happy, but then his pleasure turned to concern. "You know, Mari, I don't like your being up here alone."

"Don't worry about me. I'll be fine. Really. I'm looking forward to the peace and quiet. And I have my cell phone."

He shook his head. "You won't be able to get a signal. It's impossible in these mountains, but I had the regular service turned on for you."

"Thanks. I suppose I should give Julie the number here."

The tone of her voice suggested that giving her assistant the phone number was the last thing she wanted to do.

Mari rubbed the base of her left ring finger with her thumb, as if adjusting a ring that wasn't there.

What was that about?

He knew she'd never married. For some reason, Mrs. Newley had whispered that tidbit of information to him. Maybe she'd just broken up with someone, and that was why she was hiding at Hawk's Lake.

"If you need a fax machine, I can bring you one," he said.

"Uh…no." She ran a palm over her forehead as if she were erasing a headache. "I didn't bring a laptop, and I don't want a fax machine."

"Well, if Julie needs to send you anything important, she could always send it to my office or e-mail it to me. I'll bring it to you."

"Thanks, Brian, but that's not necessary. Just call me and I'll stop by and pick it up." She took a deep breath and let it out. "Besides, I don't want to put you out."

"Not a problem. I've done it for my renters in the past."

Mari nodded. "Let me walk you back to your car."

He felt like he was being rushed away, and that struck him as unusual. They hadn't seen each other in years. Didn't she want to catch up?

"It's good to see you again, Brian."

She looked up at him with her grass-green eyes, and a shot of warmth coursed through him.

"I was just thinking the same about you. It's been a long time, but you haven't changed much."

"I was only sixteen when you saw me last. I must have changed!"

"Okay. You're right. You're taller now, and your braces are gone." He looked her up and down. "And…a few other things have changed." Like the curves that brought an unfamiliar ache into his belly.

He remembered the day he'd realized that his pal had turned into a woman.

Suddenly, she really filled out a two-piece bathing suit, and she smelled of jasmine instead of bubble gum. She wore glittery lip gloss that he couldn't take his eyes off of. And he found himself wanting to lie next to her on the dock instead of playing basketball with the guys.

It wasn't as if he minded the new Mari. Not at all—he liked her. Maybe too much.

Shaking the memory away, Brian fished in his pocket and handed her the key. "Here you are."

"Thanks," she said. "Do you want me to sign the papers now?"

The tone of her voice signaled to him that she didn't want to sign a thing at the moment. Good. It would give him an excuse to return. He liked to make sure that his renters were comfortable. Particularly old friends who were beautiful and alone in the off-season.

But right now, he sensed that she needed to go into the cottage by herself.

"Look, I'll wait here in case you have any questions or in case you notice a problem. We'll take care of the paperwork some other time. Not much has changed. I just did some updating—the wiring, the plumbing—nothing you'd probably notice. Go ahead. Check it out, and—"

Before he could finish, she turned and walked briskly toward the house. Turning back, she threw a smile at him over her shoulder. "I'll be right back."

He couldn't remember the last time he was that

excited about anything. He loved his family, and it was great living in close proximity to them, but Mari's visit reminded him that he needed something more to make himself complete.

Seeing her and catching her up on the years that had passed reminded him of the time he'd spent living and working in New York City.

He'd attended New York University to get his MBA. While at NYU, he'd hung out at jazz clubs, noodle bars and the sidewalk cafes. In the summer, he worked at one of the bars where he knew the Wall Street crowd hung out. As part of his degree requirement, he did an internship at Banach, Grant and Wesley, a high-profile brokerage, at the recommendation of one of his professors.

He loved the fast pace at BG&W, and they loved him enough to hire him after he graduated and promote him three times.

Finally he was a player, and he was living his dream.

Five years after graduating, he received a call from his frantic sister that he was needed at home. Melanie explained that their father had had an accident at the garage, which resulted in a broken leg and wrist. The hospital was releasing him, and she couldn't take care of her father's needs, with a newborn and a husband who was always on the road. Their brother, Jack, was racing professionally and due to sponsor commitments, couldn't get away for a while.

He'd calmed Melanie down, put in for two weeks' vacation, packed up and returned to tiny, dull Hawk's Lake, where the biggest excitement was going to the Pine Cone Restaurant on a Saturday night for their pizza-and-wings buffet and listening to Big Rex and the Polka Dots play.

He kept trying to get out of town, back to the fast-paced life he'd built for himself. But something always came up to keep him in Hawk's Lake.

What could he do?

Jack was living his life as fast as he drove. Melanie needed help taking care of their dad, who was cranky because he was bored and all but totally incapacitated.

Brian couldn't just walk away. They needed him. Besides, before his mother died he'd promised her that he'd take care of the family. He made that promise, thinking that she wouldn't suffer any longer if she knew that everyone would be okay.

Finally after several years, everything and everyone was stable. Everyone had something that made them happy.

Except him.

When had he become complacent? Where had his ambitions gone?

Maybe now was the time to rekindle *his* dreams.

Chapter Three

Sherwood Lodge was as beautiful as Mari remembered. The wide mahogany floors gleamed in the late-afternoon sun, and she could see the deep, blue, spring-fed lake through the arched, beveled windows.

There was natural, beaded fir on the cathedral ceiling, accented by arched cherry trusses. This style carried through in the six bedrooms throughout the house: one on the first floor, four on the second floor and one on the third. Each bedroom either had its own screened porch or an arched, open porch.

The nearest neighbors were five hundred yards away in each direction. She'd have more than enough privacy.

Mari ran up the stairs to the turret, which had been her favorite room growing up. On rainy days, she played dolls and pretended that she was a princess in a castle, waiting for her Prince Charming—who looked remarkably like Brian Hawkins. Or she'd read a book, or write in her diary. Many times, she'd sit on the window seat and watch for someone to come over and ask her to play.

Every summer, her parents came to Sherwood Lodge for a month. Her mother and father still talked about work, and were constantly on the phone to the office, but the three of them would still find time to picnic outside and swim together. When she was younger they'd hold her hand and go for walks.

But after the month was over, her parents would return to Boston, and Grandma Rose would come and stay with her for the rest of the summer at Sherwood Lodge.

But things changed during the week of her sixteenth birthday when her father announced that they wouldn't be coming back to Hawk's Lake anymore. He'd said that he was selling Sherwood Lodge to the Hawkins family.

Mari's world came crashing down, and she'd been inconsolable. She'd barely left the turret room, and wrote endlessly in her tearstained diary. She'd constantly asked her parents why they had to sell, even begged them not to, but they held steadfast to their decision.

She remembered her father's words. "We don't really need Sherwood Lodge, Marigold. We just don't have the time to spend here. It's a simple business decision. Sometimes you have to make sacrifices."

A business decision? Her cottage wasn't a business. It was home. She wasn't alone at the lodge all the time, like she was in Boston. She was part of a family. She had parents who paid attention to her for once. Well, anyway, way more than usual.

The truth was, they'd rather work than be with her.

Because it hurt too much over the years, Mari hadn't responded to any of Melanie Hawkins's attempts to keep in touch. She and Jack hadn't really been that close, so she really didn't expect him to contact her.

But Brian was another story. He'd been her pal, then her first crush. Brian was the first boy she'd kissed. And her young heart had shattered into a million pieces when he never even said goodbye.

As time passed, the more strange it seemed to reestablish contact with any of the Hawkins kids—especially Brian—so she'd never bothered.

Looking down, she saw Brian leaning against his sporty convertible, waiting for her. He was still so handsome that she almost forgot to breathe when she looked at him.

She remembered how they used to hang out by the lake and dive off the dock. Even now, she could imagine Brian stretched out on the small piers, his sculpted body all wet and glistening in the sun....

What was she doing? This sabbatical was supposed to be about her, not a one-time crush. Touching her bare ring finger, she encouraged herself to remember that.

It wasn't about Jason Fox, either. He'd loved her—or so he said—but had only used her to get a vice president position at Sherwood. She'd given him the job, all right, then suddenly he started keeping his distance. She'd just been a tool to obtain what he wanted. How foolish she'd been to think a man would want her for herself.

She had to stick to her decision to stay away from men. Including sexy Brian Hawkins.

It was nice of him to be concerned about her staying alone, but she wasn't worried. Even though she was away from the main village and would be alone at the lake for another month or so, Hawk's Lake seemed like a place where people still didn't lock their doors.

But she'd still lock up. And not just her door— her heart was off-limits, too.

She couldn't wait to make pottery again, couldn't wait to feel the wet clay under her hands as it spun on her wheel. She wanted to take long walks in the fresh air, and watch the sun set on the lake every evening and rise every morning. And she'd enjoy biking to the village when the spirit moved her. Above all, she wanted to find *herself* again.

Brian would just be a distraction—one she couldn't afford.

Mari walked toward Brian with a happy grin, looking much more cheerful than when he'd first seen her at his real-estate office.

"Is Sherwood Lodge how you remembered it?" he asked.

"Everything is even *better* than I remembered it."

"Good."

She snapped her fingers. "The porch off the kitchen is a perfect place to put my wheel. I can put my kiln in the boathouse. Is there 220 power in there?"

Brian crossed his arms. "Yes."

"Don't worry," Mari added quickly. "I brought heavy plastic and a rug with a rubber backing. I won't harm a plank on the porch. And I won't burn down the boathouse."

He knew he should relax, but he was very protective of his properties. "I know you'll take care of the place as if it were your own."

She glanced back at the house. "I wish it still was."

He could kick himself for reminding her that the Sherwoods didn't own Sherwood Lodge anymore. "I'm sorry, Mari. That was stupid. I didn't mean to insinuate that—"

"Oh, I know." She waved her hand in dismissal. "Don't give it another thought. But I don't want to keep you, Brian. I know you have other things to do." Mari stifled a yawn. "I'm suddenly tired. Must be the fresh air. I could use a nap." She winced. "Oh, no. I forgot to bring linens."

"No problem." He went into his trunk and pulled out two plastic bags that contained two pillows, a set of queen sheets and some towels, and handed them to her. "I'm always prepared for any contingency."

"You always were. Must be the Eagle Scout in you."

He slammed the trunk shut and walked to the driver's side of his car. "What about food? Are you hungry?"

"Famished." She rubbed her forehead. "Oh, no. I was so eager to get here, I can't believe I forgot to pick up groceries, too. But I packed enough clothes for a year's stay."

Mari seemed much more relaxed. At least they were talking freely and joking a bit. He knew they hadn't parted on very good terms, but that was long ago, and he hoped that she didn't still hold that against him. He'd been young and confused about his feelings for her.

The only thing that he hadn't been confused about was his plan—a carefully laid-out plan for his future. A plan that included him taking the business world by storm. And that plan hadn't included Mari.

But in retrospect, yes, he'd been an idiot.

"Don't worry about food, Mari. The Eagle Scout comes through again. I stocked the fridge. I got you some basics, along with hot dogs and hamburgers and some frozen pizzas. It should last you a few days until you go shopping."

"Coffee?"

He nodded. "And a bottle of wine."

"You're an angel, Brian."

"Aww…thanks. But that's not what the other girls say."

"So then, you're a devil?"

He winked. "That's for me to know and you to find out."

"You are *so* thirteen years old." She rolled her eyes.

He could have stayed there all night, teasing and talking to her, but he could take a hint. Instead, he gave her a salute, climbed into his car and drove off with a friendly wave.

He'd be back tomorrow to check on her.

After Brian left, Mari was struck by the silence.

There weren't any sounds of horns blaring or construction noises. There weren't any traffic jams or people yelling, no phones ringing or faxes buzzing. There was only the gentle lapping of Hawk's Lake as it kissed the shore.

She opened the van doors and put the bags of linens in the front seat. She'd unload them later. Then she pulled out a folding lounge chair and carried it to the sandy beach at the edge of the lawn, unfolded it, got in and stretched out. As she watched the sun sparkle on the lake, she could hear the distant sound of a loon calling. Then she studied the intricate patterns on the double wings of a dragon-fly that had landed on her sleeve.

When a dragonfly landed on you, it was supposed to bring good luck. She could use some good luck.

Pulling her jacket on as the cool evening air rolled in, she watched the sun set in a blaze of red and gold, and then decided that she needed to unload some clothes from the van. After making several trips, she was done, and it was dark out. Very dark.

Her stomach growled, so she found some hot dogs in the refrigerator and put them in the micro-wave. How nice of Brian to stock the fridge for her. He'd always been sweet and thoughtful.

No. Not *always*. On her last day at Sherwood Lodge, he had hurt her to the bone.

After she ate, she grabbed a suitcase and the bags of linens that Brian had given her and climbed the stairs to her old room. Pausing at the doorway, she flicked on the light and looked around.

The windows overlooked the lake on three sides. On the right wall, there was a little screened-in porch that faced the side yard and the boathouse. She used to watch for the Hawkins kids from that window, hoping that they would ask her to come out and play.

On rainy days, she'd read a book or write in her

diary. Some nights, she'd fall asleep on the small chintz-covered couch as the gentle waves lulled her to sleep.

Mari set everything she was carrying onto the hardwood floor and walked over to the bed—her old brass bed! She ran her hand over the cool metal headboard that was decorated with sunflowers.

She remembered snuggling under the covers and listening to the murmur of her parents' voices on the porch below her.

With both of her parents downstairs, Mari felt safe and secure and totally happy. This cottage was the only place that had ever really felt like home.

Mari made up the bed, then undressed and slipped into a T-shirt and flannel pants. By the time she finished, a brisk wind was rattling the window frames. Soon, a hard rain began to pummel the roof and windows. A loud banging noise startled her, and she jumped. Over her pounding heart, she realized that it was just a loose shutter slamming against the outside of the cottage.

She slipped into bed and snuggled under a colorful, striped Hudson's Bay blanket and a fluffy beige comforter that she'd found in the hallway closet. The shutter banged again.

It was going to be a long night.

* * *

Midmorning, Brian turned down the dirt road that led to Sherwood Lodge and slowed down to dodge the puddles and potholes that had filled with water from last night's storm.

He was looking forward to seeing Mari again. It had been a long time since a woman had interested him and tweaked his curiosity, and Mari did both. Something had been missing in all the women he'd dated—something that he couldn't identify.

As a result of seeing Mari after twelve years, how beautiful and poised she'd become, he couldn't sleep last night. It was like he'd been sucker punched.

But when he thought about what she represented, that made him think about his life, and all that he'd missed. He was haunted by the realization that all his aspirations never materialized.

Was it too late for him to give his dream career another shot?

He certainly didn't begrudge Mari the success she'd achieved. Sherwood Enterprises was her family's business, just like Hawkins's Garage was his. But that was like comparing watermelons to grapes. Sure, the garage was internationally acclaimed for Mel's antique-car restoration work, and Jack's custom-built stock cars were in high demand in

North America and in Europe, but still, Sherwood Enterprises was huge—an international conglomerate.

Brian swung into the parking area near the boathouse and climbed the side stairs that led to the sunporch. He was just about to knock when Mari opened the door and jumped.

"Oh! Brian, you scared me. I didn't hear you pull up."

She was dressed in a pair of jeans and a gray Harvard sweatshirt, her hair tied back in a ponytail. She looked tired—but beautiful—and eager to start a new day. She had a book and a mug in her hands.

"I was going to go outside and read a little." She eyed his suit and tie. "Are you working today? Isn't it Saturday?"

He nodded. "I had an appointment with a man who is being audited by the IRS on Monday. He and his lawyer wanted my opinion."

She did an exaggerated shiver, and he laughed.

"Did you help him?" she asked.

"I believe so."

"Did you do his taxes originally?"

"No. If I did, he never would have been audited."

"Now that's confidence. Maybe I should get you to do the taxes for Sherwood. We always get audited."

"Just say the word, and I'm there." He couldn't believe those words had come out of his mouth.

"If I thought you were serious, I'd take you up on that."

Even though he wanted to do more than taxes if he were ever hired at Sherwood, Mari didn't really mean that she'd hire him. She probably thought of him as just a small-town CPA.

She took a sip of coffee and smiled. "By the way, landlord, I didn't get much sleep last night. There was a loose shutter banging in the wind."

"I'll take a look and fix it."

"Thanks." She pointed to the folder in his hand. "Is that for me to sign?"

He gave her the folder and a pen. "I can go through it with you. We could do a joint inspection."

"No need. The cottage is perfect, or it will be, when you fix the shutter. And I sign several contracts a day. I can manage a little thing like this." She glanced down at the papers.

Whoa! That was a reminder that his *little* contract and routine forms were less than insignificant in her world.

Maybe that wasn't how she'd meant it. He was just being too sensitive, due to her success and his lack of it.

He might as well fix the shutter and head back to the village.

"I have some sweats in the car. I'll fix the shutter so it won't bother you again. Mind if I use the bathroom to change?"

"No. And thanks, Brian," she said over her shoulder, walking toward her lawn chair.

He headed for his car, taking deep breaths and counting slowly to ten. What he really wanted to do was head to the gym and let off some frustration, or jog up the logging trail that twisted around Mist Mountain.

Maybe then he'd sweat out the real reasons he hadn't gone back to Wall Street. The feelings of guilt and responsibility he'd carried for years—a burden that had long since dimmed his dreams.

He changed his clothes and put his suit into his car. Then he found a ladder in the storage barn, dusted the cobwebs off it with an old corn broom and lugged it to the cottage.

Glancing over at Mari, he saw that she had the folder open and was looking at his contract. Correction: his *little* contract.

He swore under his breath. It wasn't Mari's fault that he'd pretty much given up on his dreams. He had no one to blame but himself.

He was just about to step onto the roof when a duck flew low over Mari, quacking loudly.

She screamed and rolled off the lawn chair, hitting the ground facedown. Papers flew everywhere.

He tried not to smile as he climbed down the ladder to see if she was okay. Just as he reached her, she lifted her head and began to laugh. He helped her up and wasn't prepared for the way his nerve endings started to tingle when he touched her arms. He pulled her up and into his arms to steady her. Their foreheads touched as she looked down at her wet, muddy clothes.

"That was a duck, wasn't it?" she asked.

He grinned. "Uh-huh."

She didn't move from his arms, but seemed to feel comfortable.

She still chuckled, and he could feel each movement of her body against his. "Do you know how dumb I feel right now?" she asked.

"I've got a good idea."

Any resentment that was still churning inside him faded when he saw Mari's smile and heard her laugh.

"If you tell anyone that I was scared by a duck, I'll deny it."

"Pirate promise." He put his index finger and thumb to his lips and made like he was turning a key and throwing it away over his shoulder. It was their old childhood pledge, a vow made whenever they were sure they would get into trouble for something they'd done.

"Pirate promise," she mumbled, staring at his lips.

Suddenly, his mouth went dry and he couldn't swallow. Then she blinked and turned away.

He took a deep breath and let it out. What was she trying to do to him?

"I can't believe you remembered that." Her voice seemed far away, as if she were thinking out loud.

"Of course I do."

She blinked. "Well, I should probably get out of these muddy clothes," she said, moving away to pick up the papers and slip them into the folder. Handing it to him, she said, "They're a bit wet, but they're signed."

"Okay." He put the folder onto her lounge chair and wove it under and over a couple of straps to keep it from blowing away. "I'll get it later. I'd better get back to the shutter."

As he turned to walk away, Mari reached out to stop him. Before she touched him, she quickly dropped her hand.

"Brian, I suppose you're wondering what I'm

doing in Hawk's Lake after twelve years," she said quietly.

He nodded. "It had crossed my mind."

"I was always happy here—mostly," she said quietly, looking out at the water.

"We did have a great time when we were kids," he said truthfully. "I couldn't wait till you got here every summer." He purposely avoided addressing the reason why she wasn't *completely* happy here. It was because of him.

He thought about their first kiss, and how sweet and warm her lips tasted—like blueberries and sunshine. Her eyes widened, and he knew that she was remembering the same moment.

"The summers that I spent here were wonderful," she said. "They were the best times of my life, and I want to do it all again. That's one of the reasons I'm here now."

He realized that it was the best time of his childhood, too, mostly due to Mari.

Whenever they were together, he could be himself. He'd share his dreams of leaving Hawk's Lake and making a name for himself in the business world, and Mari wouldn't laugh, like his sister or brother would.

"You can do it, Bri," she'd always said. "I know you can."

Talking with Mari fed his soul, and he'd feel like he was on top of the world.

His adventures with Mari fed his spirit. Along with their endless pirate scenarios, they solved imaginary mysteries, caught enough bad guys to fill two prisons and saved the lives of many innocents.

And just before Mari went back to Boston for good, he'd lost his heart to her.

The thought of saying goodbye hurt too much—so he didn't. He took the easy way out and accepted a job at a sleep-away camp in a nearby town, where he spent the remainder of the summer.

It had been a long time since he'd gone swimming in the lake, or taken a boat ride just for the fun of it. He hadn't fished or waterskied in years. Why not? The lake was just yards from the front yard of Hawk's Roost, his family's camp up the lake. He didn't even have time for golf, and his town house was on the second fairway of a golf course. His life was his work, and had been for quite some time.

But Mari's excitement was contagious, and suddenly he felt the urge to rediscover the fun of all those things with her, and more.

"It's a little cold right now for swimming, but it'll be okay in a month or so," he said. "In the meantime, we could hike, go on a few picnics. I could find us a couple of bikes, and—"

She laid a hand on his arm. "You don't understand."

"What don't I understand?"

Mari sighed. "I'm sorry, Brian. I'd love to do all those things and more. But I came to Hawk's Lake because I was going through a rough patch and needed to get away from everything—my job, Boston and men in general." She paused and gave him a weak smile. "I hope you understand, but I need to figure out my life and make some decisions. And I can't afford any distractions."

Brian's smile faded. "I get it. You want me to leave you alone."

Chapter Four

Mari flushed and realized she'd totally bungled her explanation.

Brian wanted to re-create the fun times of her childhood for her, and she was being an ungrateful jerk.

He looked down at her as if she'd just slapped him. In a way, she had.

"It's not you," she added quickly. "And it's not that I wouldn't like to see more of you and catch up, but…"

She faltered. He didn't need to know all this. Besides, she didn't know what more to say without sounding presumptive. He wasn't asking her out on a date, he was just being nice.

Brian yanked off his sweatshirt, and she caught a glimpse of his muscled stomach before he tugged down a bright blue T-shirt. She cast her eyes to the lake to avoid looking at him.

"I understand." He waved away any further explanation and began climbing the ladder. "But trust me, Mari. A couple of weeks alone out here, and you'll be screaming for company."

Brian found the offending shutter. The eye of the hook-and-eye catch was missing, the part that held it to the house. In the winter, the shutters could be hooked together over the windows to block out snow and wind. There was nothing he could do right now other than nail the shutter to the house, and there was no way he was going to do that. Or he could tap out the hinges, if he had the tools.

But he didn't, so Mari would just have to live with the shutter whacking against the house until he could get the part.

A big chunk of him was ticked. Here he was, trying to make her return to Hawk's Lake as perfect and as convenient as possible, and she was basically telling him to hit the road.

Well, that was an exaggeration. She'd come here on vacation, and for some fun, not to support *his* sudden zest for activity.

Brian climbed down the ladder and put his tools away, ready to head back to his office in the village.

If she wanted to be alone, that was her prerogative, but he was still disappointed.

He fired up his Mustang, and was just about to back up when he caught a movement out of the corner of his eye. He turned and saw the lift on the side of the van lowering to the ground. Mari stood on it, holding a red dolly with what he assumed was her pottery wheel balanced precariously on it.

She was going to hurt herself. He turned off his car and hurried toward the van. "Why didn't you yell for me?"

"I didn't want to bother you, and I thought I could do it myself. But it's a little awkward."

"It's not balanced." He took the handle of the dolly from her.

"I can do it—"

"Alone," he finished. "Yes, I know." He yanked on the strap of the belt to tighten it more. "But I want to help you."

She opened her mouth to say something, but

shook her head and started walking ahead of him, dodging puddles as she crossed the road and headed to the side door.

With her pottery wheel in tow, Brian walked behind her, trying to ignore the sway of her hips as she walked and the tug of her jeans across her backside. The woman was tying him in knots, making him crazy. And she'd *just arrived.*

As soon as he could get away from her, he'd go back to his office and regroup. He was handling everything badly today.

As he pulled the dolly up the steps and onto the side porch, he saw that Mari had laid down clear, thick plastic and a big striped rug. There were neatly stacked bags containing different shades of clay, along with an aluminum bucket overflowing with sponges and what were probably pottery tools.

"I'll make sure that I contain the mess," she said.

He set her wheel down in the middle of the room where she pointed.

"So, what does it take to be a potter?" he asked.

Her face changed. The worry lines on her forehead faded, and her mouth dissolved into a smile. She became animated, alive.

"It takes imagination to find what's hiding inside a lump of clay and bring it out. Then once I do, I can shape and glaze the piece and fire it and make it my own. There's nothing like it in the world."

He couldn't help being mesmerized by the dreamy expression on her face. All too soon, she noticed him looking at her. The glow disappeared and a stiff, self-conscious smile took its place.

"Can we unload my kiln now?" she said, averting her eyes.

It seemed like it pained her to ask him for help. He was just about to touch the small of her back, just to escort her back to the van, but she moved away. He'd meant it only as friendly gesture, and never expected that kind of response. Why was she so jumpy?

As they walked to the van in silence, he made sure to leave an ample amount of space between them.

Once there, he tied the kiln securely onto the dolly. It was smaller than he'd expected, and much lighter. He rolled it into the boathouse, set it in place where Mari directed and plugged it in for her.

"You're all set. I'll pick up the part I need for the shutter, and be back to fix it in a couple of days."

"Thanks, Brian. I'd appreciate it."

As he drove back to his town house, he wondered who had hurt Mari so much that she was determined to sequester herself in the woods.

* * *

Mari watched as Brian drove down the muddy road and disappeared from sight.

Maybe now she could relax.

She couldn't help but feel that the accountant in him didn't miss a thing. It was as if he'd totaled everything up and found her lacking.

Well, what did he expect? She was no longer the girl who gathered wildflowers in the meadow, or who rode her bike down Sunrise Hill with her hands and feet in the air.

She was president of Sherwood Enterprises, Inc., a major corporation. She had duties and responsibilities that few could imagine. The livelihoods of over three thousand people depended on her business acumen and insight. And she was the last in a long line of men and women—mostly women—who had built Sherwood from a one-woman pottery business to the powerhouse that it was today.

Yes, she was in Hawk's Lake to find herself, but she didn't need Brian Hawkins to remind her of those heavenly, happy-go-lucky days. Nor did she want to be attracted to him, or feel his touch, even if it was simply a friendly gesture.

She was vulnerable right now, and it didn't help that she'd thought about him over the years, wondered what he was doing, if he'd ever married or had children. Never in her wildest dreams did she think he'd turn out as handsome as he had—or that he still could make her heart do flips in her chest.

But he was the one who had crushed her young teenage heart. The one who made her extra careful of giving her heart away. And ever since, when she finally did fall for someone, it never seemed to work out.

What was wrong with her?

Mari walked into the sunporch. It felt good to have her wheel ready to go, and her kiln in the boathouse. She couldn't wait to feel what it was like to have her hands all muddy and wet, creating something from scratch.

She looked at her perfectly manicured nails and grinned. They wouldn't look so perfect tomorrow morning when she reintroduced herself to her wheel.

For two days, Mari was alone, and she forced herself not to think of Brian or Sherwood Enterprises. She just enjoyed working on her wheel and living in the moment.

Six pots of various sizes sat drying on a table that she'd covered loosely with newspaper. None of them were as good as they could be, yet the happy memory of Grandma Rose teaching her was just as vivid now as it was when it was happening.

They had sat on this very porch. Gram had her arms around her. "Feel the clay, Mari dear. And when it's ready, you can pull it up. Be careful. Not too much water, or it'll flop over. There you go. Perfect! You're a natural—just like the other Sherwood women."

Then they'd cut it off the wheel with a wire to dry. Mari couldn't wait to fire it to bisque and then paint it with various glazes. When Gram opened the kiln, it was like coming downstairs on Christmas morning and seeing the gifts all gaily wrapped under the tree—a wonderful surprise.

"It's just beautiful, Marigold," Gram would say, studying one of her pieces. "If your great-grandmother Lily could see this, she'd be so proud."

Lily's mother, Violet Sherwood, had started Sherwood Enterprises, originally named Sherwood Pottery, in the carriage house behind her old Victorian in Stockbridge, Massachusetts. Over the years their bestselling china patterns and corresponding accessories were named after the Sherwood women: Violet, Lily, Rose and Marigold.

If Mari didn't take over the reins at Sherwood, it would be the end of the family's control of the corporation.

She couldn't let that happen. Yet the thought of managing the family business forever—not to mention the pressure—was making her miserable.

She wanted children—a bunch of them—but there was no way she wanted to bring them up the way she'd been brought up—by absentee parents. Parents who were too busy running and expanding their company to pay much attention to a lonely little girl.

Briefly, she thought of her office and closed her eyes. Here at the lake, there was no intercom. No e-mails to answer, no calls to return. No lengthy meetings to attend—nor a million other minute details to handle.

It was calm, peaceful and silent.

As if reading her mind, the phone rang, startling her. Hurrying to the kitchen, she found herself hoping it was Brian Hawkins.

"Hello?"

"Mari! It's Melanie Hawkins. Welcome back to Hawk's Lake."

Mari sat down on one of the kitchen chairs and smiled.

"Mel!" It was wonderful to hear the voice of her childhood friend. "How are you?"

"Anxious to catch up with you. I called to invite

you over for a small party tomorrow—a birthday party—for my my son, Kyle."

Mari hesitated for only a moment. Sure, she wanted to discover herself again and to think about her life, but she wasn't going to pass up a chance to reconnect with old friends.

"I'd love to come, Melanie."

Two hours later, Mari pulled her van into a parking space in front of Clancy's grocery store.

To call Clancy's a "grocery store" was a misnomer. It was more like ten stores rolled into one. Sure, there were groceries, but where the beverage aisle ended, sporting goods started. Bait was sold in a corner by the rods and reels.

One wing housed clothes for every member of the family—another, books and yarn and crafts. Seasonal decorations took up still another area, and Mari could see decorated Christmas trees in the same space as jack-o'-lanterns and black cats. Toys for all ages took up two long aisles, pots and pans and kitchen items took up three. There were boats for sale outside on the right of the building, snowmobiles on the left. A sign over the front door proclaimed, If we don't have it, it hasn't been made yet—the perfect motto for Clancy's.

Mari reminded herself to buy some groceries, a birthday gift for Kyle and some nail polish to repair her nails. She wanted to look her best at the party.

She told herself that it wasn't because of Brian, but in her heart, she knew she was lying.

It wasn't the first time.

Strolling the aisles, she picked out several items that she needed, and even more that she didn't. Compared to Boston, it was hard to resist the prices.

As she pushed her cart past the baby clothes, she decided that she'd like to buy something for Angeline, Melanie's eight-month-old baby.

Mari handled every dress, every hair accessory and every pair of socks with lace trim. She was delighted for Melanie, who sounded so full of joy as she spoke of Angeline and Kyle.

As happy as she was for her friend, whenever Mari thought about how she might not ever have any children, a deep sadness settled inside her.

But she was afraid to take that CEO job and try to raise a family at the same time. After all, her parents hadn't been able to balance the business and their child. What made her think she'd be any different?

"Oh!" she said, finding a smocked sundress with rosebuds and a little white crocheted jacket. "This is just too cute." Even more adorable was a bonnet, which, when tied, would form the petals of a sun-flower around Angeline's face. Mari added pink tights, soft, white shoes and a little stuffed lamb.

As she picked out some grocery items, she couldn't remember the last time she'd spent such an enjoyable time shopping. The creaky wooden floors under her sandals and the absence of people made the experience enjoyable. She covered every square inch and covered it again, just to make sure she hadn't missed anything. Just as she was checking out, a deep voice rang out.

"Hi, Mari!"

Her heart did a flip, and she scanned the store. She saw Brian at one of the checkouts.

"Hi, there." He looked striking in a golf shirt, a blue that brought out the turquoise in his eyes and that stretched across his broad chest. He wore tan khakis that fit him perfectly. A brown leather belt cinched his waist.

"Can I help you with those groceries?" he asked, eyeing her mountain of bags.

As he came closer, she could smell his after-shave—the clean scent of pine and spice. "I can manage, Brian, but thanks anyway. Aren't you working today?"

He nodded and held up a paper bag. "I needed a

couple of things for the office." He snapped his fingers. "Which reminds me. I got a fax for you from Julie about an hour ago."

"I'll pick it up on my way home. Thanks." They left the store and he started down the sidewalk. "Do you want a ride?"

He smiled. "On a gorgeous day like this? I'll walk."

"See you in a bit."

She opened the back door of the van, but instead of putting her purchases inside, she watched Brian walk away.

He turned back suddenly, and caught her staring. Grinning, he waved.

Busted.

Her cheeks heated as she lifted her hand in a weak acknowledgment, then concentrated on emptying her cart.

Several minutes later, Mari entered Brian's office. Mrs. Newley wasn't there, but Brian was at his desk, on the phone. He motioned for her to come on back.

She lifted the counterpiece that acted as a barrier between the waiting area and the workplace, walked back to his glass-enclosed office and took a seat.

Brian smiled at her, put his hand over the mouthpiece of the phone and whispered, "Hang on a minute. I have to ask you something." He handed her a stack of papers.

It was her fax from Julie. Glancing at it, she saw that it was nothing that couldn't have waited until she returned—just some monthly stats and reports from various department heads.

She smiled back at Brian and skimmed the material. He'd no sooner hung up the phone than it rang again.

"Sorry," he said. "I'm waiting to hear about an offer on a vacant building for an anxious client, or I'd let the machine get it."

"No problem."

As she skimmed the fax, her eyes kept returning to Brian. He was much more interesting and definitely in his element. He fielded his calls with confidence, knowledge and an easygoing demeanor that would equal or surpass any executives at Sherwood.

Again he hung up, and again the phone rang. "I'm sorry. It's normally not this busy."

"Don't be silly," Mari said. "For a change, I've got all the time in the world."

Through the open windows, she could see some children playing jump rope on the sidewalk.

She could hear the girls giggle, and she could

smell the sweetness of fresh-cut grass as a lawn mower droned in the distance.

In contrast, her office windows in Boston were sealed shut. All she could see were other office buildings—a soaring mix of glass and brick and gray cement.

Finally, he hung up the phone. "Sorry about the wait. Hopefully, that'll be it for a while."

"I know how it feels. My phone at work never stops ringing, and it's impossible to get anything done. I just hate it."

"I love it." He grinned. "It gets my blood pumping."

She stood to leave.

"Mari, would you like to go with me to my nephew's seventh birthday tomorrow?"

She was just about to tell him that Melanie had already invited her when he held up his hand.

"I know you want to be alone, but my family wants to see you. I promise you it'll be fun. It's just a barbecue, and probably a campfire at night." He tapped a pencil on the desk, and Mari wondered if he was anxious that she'd say no.

"Melanie already asked me to come, Brian."

"Oh, I didn't know that. I haven't talked to her today." He let out a deep breath. "And what did you say?"

"I said I'd love to."

Smiling, his turquoise eyes lit up. "I'm glad."

Suddenly, things seemed awkward between them. It wasn't as if it was a date or anything like that....

"Well, I'd better get my groceries home." Standing, she was about to pick up her reports that she'd laid on his desk, just as he did the same. Brian's hand brushed against hers and lingered. It was warm and strong—just like him. She pulled away reluctantly.

"Can I give you a ride to Mel's?" Brian said.

"That's not necessary. I can drive myself."

"Let me pick you up, Mari. Then you won't have to worry about finding her house, and you can enjoy the ride."

"Okay," she relented. "I'm looking forward to it. And I can't wait to see her new baby, and everyone else for that matter."

But she had to admit to herself that it was Brian that she really couldn't wait to see again.

Outside, she stopped to watch the girls playing jump rope. She remembered being one of the best jumpers in Boston.

"Jump in," said the girl whose turn it was next.

Mari hesitated. "It's been a long time."

"You can do it. My mother does it."

Sheesh. "Okay." Mari put her purse on the lawn. She couldn't help but glance up and see Brian standing at the window. He gave her a thumbs-up.

She grinned and shrugged. "Ready?" She watched the rope go round and round, and found herself swaying like she used to, waiting for the perfect opportunity to jump in. Then she was off. But the rope hit her foot.

"Try it again, lady," said the other rope twirler.

She did, and this time she succeeded. She jumped in the middle of the rope and lost count of how many times. She turned around in the middle, and the girls went a little faster…then faster.

She kept up, laughing, until she made the mistake of looking over at Brian. They locked gazes, and she lost her timing. She stumbled as the rope snagged the tip of her shoe, throwing her off balance. Catching herself, she could see that Brian had started toward her, obviously concerned that she might have been hurt.

When he saw that she was okay, he waved and smiled.

Breathing heavily, she thanked the girls, then turned again to Brian. He was clapping. She did a curtsy, picked up her purse and walked to the van, feeling happier than she had in a long time.

Chapter Five

Brian pulled into the driveway behind Sherwood Lodge and saw Mari sitting on the patio, staring at the lake. Beside her was a plastic bin overflowing with brightly wrapped gifts.

She turned and put a finger over her lips. He walked quietly over to her and sat down.

"Aren't they cute?" she whispered, pointing at the beach.

Six ducklings were huddled around their mother, taking a nap in the sun.

He was so used to the cycle of life around the

lake, he usually took it for granted. "Cute," he agreed, looking at the mother and ducklings and seeing them through Mari's eyes. "I think she could be the duck who dived at you. She must have been in a hurry to get back to the family."

"I thought she looked familiar." Mari chuckled. "I could watch them all day, but we should probably get going."

As if on cue, the ducks woke up and waddled off toward the lake.

Yet Mari didn't make a move to leave.

Brian noticed that, during her brief time here, Mari was looking better already. She seemed to have more energy, more color in her cheeks.

"Mari, why did you really come back to Hawk's Lake?"

She folded her hands in her lap. "I told you. I needed a vacation."

"But what else? Did something happen in Boston? Are you okay?"

"Well…" She looked down at her ring finger, then up at the sky, as if the answer was written there. "I'm okay."

He waited, but she didn't elaborate. "Is there anything I can help with?"

She sighed. "If anyone could understand, Brian,

it's you. You work in your family's business, just like I do. You take care of the books at the garage and all, and—"

He nodded. "Sometimes it can be tough, working in a family business."

Her eyes met his, and he could see the anguish in them.

"Absolutely," Mari agreed. "Especially if you're an only child like me."

He nodded. "Or if your siblings have problems of their own to deal with, and you have to pick up the slack."

"Or if you're the last of the line," she said.

"Or if you have dreams of your own that have been pushed to the back burner," Brian replied.

"Yes!" she agreed. "Or if you've just broken up with a man."

"Or... *What?*" Brian raised an eyebrow. "Sorry. That never happened to me."

She laughed, then lowered her eyes. "He's not worth talking about."

"To be honest, I suspected something like that."

She raised an eyebrow.

"You tend to look down at your left hand, or touch a ring that isn't there." He met her gaze. "Was it serious?"

"I thought so. Matter of fact, I thought so three times."

He couldn't help himself from reaching for her hand and holding it, and for once, she didn't pull away.

"Forget them. None of them deserved a woman like you." He thought he saw the hint of tears in the corners of her eyes. He wanted to ask her more, to find out how the bastard had hurt her, but it was too private a pain.

"Thank you for that," she said.

"Now, cheer up. We're going to have a great time at Mel's." He'd show her a good time, and she'd forget about *him.*

He pointed to the plastic bin of gifts. "You shouldn't have done that."

"It was fun," she said. "They're all little things. I have an idea for a little surprise—a game."

"That's very thoughtful of you. Kyle and his friends will love it." He picked up the bin, and they walked to his car.

On the way to Melanie's house, they kept up a steady chatter. "Do you remember Sunshine Cottage?" he asked.

"It was your house. Right?"

"Yes, and my grandparents' house before us. Melanie always loved that house, and she lives there now. Her husband, Sam, loves it, too. He said it reminds him of his childhood home in Canada."

When they pulled in, Melanie ran out with an excited scream and scooped Mari into a big hug.

"Mel, you're taller, of course, but I would know you anywhere." Mari grinned. "It's good to see you."

"This is my husband, Sam," Melanie said proudly. She smoothed the baby's blanket. "And this little doll is Angeline. Angie for short. And this adorable guy is Kyle, who is seven today."

"Oh, Mom!" said Kyle, blushing to the roots of his sandy-brown hair.

Mari cooed over Angeline, and took the time to ask Kyle a few questions and wish him a happy birthday.

Brian caught the expression of longing on Mari's face when she looked at the kids.

"Are you Uncle Brian's girlfriend?" Kyle asked.

Brian held his breath. It figured that Kyle would ask such a thing.

Mari smiled. "I'm an old friend. I used to play with your mother and uncles when we were kids. My parents used to own Sherwood Lodge, and I came here every summer."

"You don't look that old," Kyle said, then ran off to greet his grandfather and Uncle Jack, who'd just pulled in.

"Do you want to hold Angeline?" Sam asked Mari. "I have a couple of things I have to do before Melanie yells at me."

"That's right." Melanie laughed. "Get to work."

"I'd love to, Sam," Mari said. "But I really don't know how. I mean, I haven't been around many babies."

"I didn't have any experience until now, either," Sam said, handing Angeline over to Mari. "Just support her head."

Sam showed her, and within seconds Mari looked as though she was born to the job. Her eyes got all dreamy, and she had a contemplative expression on her face when she looked at Angeline.

"I am so glad you're here, Mari," Melanie said, putting her arm around Mari's shoulder. "I can't wait to catch up with you. It's been so long."

As they walked toward the party, talking excitedly, Brian got the packages out of the car and carried them to the side yard of the big yellow house, up the stairs to a big deck that was decorated with balloons and streamers.

Kyle and his friends were playing kick ball on the expansive lawn.

Brian pulled out a chair for Mari and the baby and sat down next to her. There was a lot of chatter as everyone exchanged greetings with his father, Ed Hawkins, and Jack. He offered to take Angie, but Mari wouldn't hear of it. She seemed content just to sit and rub the baby's back.

Every so often, she'd whisper to Angie, who was curled up against Mari's shoulder, cooing and dozing.

Brian could have watched Mari forever—the wonder on her face when she looked at the baby, the happy sparkle in her eyes, the little motherly gestures and the sounds she made. He wondered why he was noticing every little thing about her—he'd certainly never paid this much attention to any other woman holding a baby.

"You're a natural, Mari. You'd make a great mother."

"Maybe," she said quietly. "But finding a father might be difficult. My choice of men hasn't been all that great."

Her words struck a chord of regret in Brian. Any man who would hurt Mari was a fool.

Yet he was the biggest fool of them all. He was the one who'd hurt her first.

Mari hated to give up Angeline, even though her arms ached, but it was time for Melanie to feed her.

It was good to be around such a close family,

observing how they related to one another, enjoyed each other's company.

If this were *her* family, her mother would be on her cell phone, and her father would be sending e-mails on his BlackBerry. There would certainly never be a treasure hunt.

She turned to Brian. "Come with me. I have a present to hide in the woods for Kyle to find. I cleared it with Melanie and Sam. I wanted to make sure it was okay with them."

"Sure," he said. "Sounds interesting."

When they tried to disappear quietly, so as not to pique Kyle's curiosity, Jack and the other men made some teasing comments as to what they were going to do.

"What *are* we doing?" Brian asked.

"Well, I put a treasure map in Kyle's birthday card, and—" Melanie pulled out a metal box from her purse. "We are hiding pirate's treasure for Kyle to find. Inside are gold-wrapped chocolate coins, gum and some other little things I've picked up."

"He'll love it," Brian said.

"I know I did when I was his age. Remember how we used to make a treasure map, and the other person had to follow it?"

"That's what I was just thinking." He chuckled.

"Remember how you made a treasure chest out of a cigar box and—"

"And I covered it with silver and gold glitter glue. And I glued on some pennies and nickels."

"You gave it to me, and I'd make the treasure map, and we'd put our treasures into your box," he finished.

Brian took her elbow and helped her through an uneven patch of land. She could feel his strength as he guided her, and she thought that she should have worn sneakers instead of fancy Italian wedge heels so his help wouldn't have been necessary.

"The treasure map that I'm giving to Kyle was one that you'd made," she said.

He looked at her in amazement. "You've kept one of my maps all this time?"

She chuckled. "I've kept every pirate map that you've ever made—in my old diaries."

He stopped and turned toward her. "And you brought them with you?"

"Yes." She looked up at him. "And before you ask me why, the answer is for old-time's sake. I just wish I hadn't lost that treasure chest. I don't know what happened to it."

"I wonder what else is in your old diaries. Anything about me?" He raised an eyebrow.

"Oh, yes. You were the star."

"Was I the star of a comedy or a tragedy?" he asked, taking both her hands.

"Both." She looked deep into his eyes, her smile fading. "You broke my heart, you know."

"I know," he said softly. "I didn't mean to, but you were too young, and I was too—"

"Immature?"

"Probably. But I was really falling for you, Mari." He swallowed hard. "I hurt you, and that was the last thing I wanted to do."

She wanted to ask him why he hadn't called, hadn't written. But she found herself standing too close to him, and they were gazing into each other's eyes.

They were going to kiss, and finally something in the back of her mind sounded an alarm. She couldn't let him—*shouldn't* let him. She'd come here to get away from her life, and here she was, falling into old habits again, drawn to a man too easily.

As she gazed into his eyes, she could hear children's laughter in the distance. Kyle's party was in progress, and it reminded her that they were supposed to be hiding his gifts. The metal box from Clancy's dug into the palm of her hand, bringing her back to the present.

They pulled away at the same time.

"Um…" Brian's hands were back at his sides.

Mari bent down and hid the box under a pile of leaves at the base of an old cement property stake, hoping Brian couldn't see her blushing.

"This is just where you hid my butterfly pin," she said, trying to make things lighter.

"And you found it in less than a half hour."

She put her hands on her hips. "Well, I never said that your maps were difficult."

They laughed, and they were back to their old selves again—almost. She'd softened toward him.

But while Mari reminded herself yet again not to get involved with Brian, she wasn't sure she could control the heat that he awakened inside her.

Brian couldn't believe that he'd almost kissed Mari.

She was on the rebound and had made it perfectly clear that she wanted to be left alone—that she wasn't interested in anything more than friendship.

Brian knew she'd come to the party to see everyone and catch up—certainly not for him. In a way, that was disappointing.

He had no good excuse for not calling her or writing her, other than that he'd had plans for himself—big plans. And he just hadn't been ready—or willing—to give up his dreams.

But he could never explain this to her now. He'd seem so shallow, so arrogant. Basically, he'd picked his ambition over a friend. No, not a friend. The girl he could have—might have—loved.

They rejoined the group, and Kyle opened his presents. The pirate costume that Mari had given him was the envy of his pals, and the subsequent treasure hunt was a huge success with the kids.

Angeline was once again snuggled on Mari's shoulder, and Mari was eating a hamburger with one hand. Brian's father had her ear and was regaling her with stories of the "old days" on Hawk's Lake, when Ezra Hawkins established a smithy here and the town was slowly built around it.

When his sister finally scooped up Angie to put her to bed, Brian could see the disappointment on Mari's face.

By the time Melanie returned with a baby monitor in her hand, the sun was setting, and Jack and Sam had a fire blazing in the ring. Kyle and his friends were sitting on big logs and had marshmallows on sticks ready to toast.

Melanie put her hand on his shoulder. "Bri, I meant to tell you, but I've had some trouble with

Buzz's Antique Auto Parts. They keep sending me the wrong fenders for the '32 Ford."

"Don't worry about it, sis. I'll take care of it in the morning, and you'll have your fenders in two days."

"Thanks, Brian. I knew I could count on you."

Jack snapped his fingers. "That reminds me. Brian, I have to ship a stock car to New Hampshire so Bobby Regent can test drive it while he's out there. He's interested in buying it. I'd like to use a different company than the Killborn Brothers. Do you have any ideas?"

"I do. I have the contact information in my office at the garage, and…" Brian sighed. "How about if I just make the arrangements for you?"

Jack grinned. "I was hoping you'd say that. Thanks."

Brian pulled out a BlackBerry from his back pocket and made a few quick notes, then leaned back in his Adirondack chair and put his hands behind his head. He had a lot of things to take care of tomorrow. He'd better get up early and get to it.

Mari put her hand on the arm of his chair. "Brian, I can't remember when I had such a good time. It must be nice to have such a close family."

He laughed. "Without them, life in Hawk's Lake would really be dull."

"You think so?" she asked.

"I know so. Truthfully, I think you're lucky to live in Boston," he said.

"You've got to be kidding."

"It's an exciting city—just like New York. I loved it when I lived there. Now, that's an incredible place. There was always something to do. In Hawk's Lake, they roll the sidewalks up at five o'clock."

Mari shrugged. "That's good. Then everyone can go home to their families."

He'd never thought of that.

"And don't forget our magnificent stores," he joked. "Like Clancy's."

"Brian, Clancy's is the most incredible place. You can find everything you want in one stop. And you can walk or drive anyplace you need to go and park for free, just steps from any business here. No commuting headaches."

"I can see I'm losing this argument," Brian said.

"You can't say anything bad about Hawk's Lake to me. I couldn't wait to get back here. I'm just disappointed that I didn't return sooner."

"I'm disappointed, too," he said.

"You are?"

"Of course."

He took her hand and kissed the back of it. His

brother, Jack, gave a long, low whistle. Brian had forgotten that they weren't alone—that everyone was around the campfire and all eyes were on them. Kyle and his friends were laughing. Melanie looked like a deer caught in headlights. Sam and Ed exchanged knowing glances.

What was he doing?

He dropped her hand and looked up at the sky. "It's a little cloudy. On a clear evening, I should take you out on the lake. The view is amazing."

She leaned over to him and whispered, "So there *is* something you like about Hawk's Lake after all?"

"One thing." He smiled. "And you make it two."

"You don't have to walk me into the cottage," Mari said as Brian pulled up to Sherwood Lodge later that night. "I'm fine."

She didn't want him to kiss her at the door, nor did she want to invite him in.

Okay…maybe she did.

She should have known that she'd be attracted to him again. But it was probably only because she was still vulnerable after the Jason Fox incident.

No. That wasn't it. She and Brian just couldn't pick up where they'd left off—when she was sixteen and he was eighteen, and they came within a blink of making love.

Too much time had gone by, and she wasn't the same innocent girl anymore.

Besides, if she decided to take the CEO job, she would probably never return to Hawk's Lake. She'd be busier than ever.

And if she didn't take the job, she'd break her parents' and Grandma Rose's hearts.

"Thanks, Brian. I had a really wonderful time." Since it was a little after midnight, she didn't have to fake a yawn to get away.

The clouds had finally passed. Now the moon was shining on the lake, and the water was sparkling in the glow. She could see her way to the side porch door.

He got out of the car anyway, appeared at her side and opened the door. Brian was always a gentleman.

"I wouldn't want you to run into any skunks or bears."

She laughed. "I'd forgotten about those critters."

"Another negative to add to the tally of Hawk's Lake."

"But they're cute. And we're the intruders. Not them," Mari pointed out.

His eyes twinkled in amusement. She just loved his eyes.

"If you don't mind, I'd like to fix the shutter tomorrow. It won't take long. Then I'll be out of your hair."

"Tomorrow is good. I'm going to go for a walk and work on my pottery. Maybe write a little in my journal."

He slid his hands into his pockets. "Sounds like a busy day."

"Sounds like a *relaxing* day. You should try it sometime. Melanie told me that you're always busy working. Jack and Ed, and even Sam, agreed with her."

He grimaced. "They should know. They're the ones who always have something for me to do."

"I did notice tonight that Melanie and Jack seemed very dependent on you. But you were the one who jumped to volunteer to help them out— which they obviously expected you to do."

"I jumped to volunteer?"

"Yes, you did. So you can't blame them entirely." As she slid out of the seat, she thought that tonight probably wasn't an isolated incident, and that Brian's family was used to him taking charge when they didn't want to deal with something. But that was the kind of guy he'd always been. He'd help anyone who asked—or didn't quite come out and ask—for his help. "Thanks again, Brian. It was so wonderful to see everyone again and get caught up. And it was a real treat holding Angie."

"I thought you were going to kidnap her."

She laughed. "I wanted to."

"You looked really...beautiful...holding her."

How would she ever respond to a touching statement like that?

Brian would make a remarkable father. She'd watched him on the treasure hunt, pretending to give them wrong clues, like he didn't want the kids finding the treasure. He'd had just as good a time as they had.

And whenever he talked to Angie, her bright blue eyes would grow wide, and happy gurgles would erupt from her tiny mouth.

"So, how come a handsome, eligible bachelor like you never married?"

He shrugged. "Hawk's Lake doesn't exactly have a wild singles' scene."

He walked her to the door, and she stood on the bottom step. She hated moments like these. To kiss or not to kiss?

She was just about to lean over when he gave her a quick peck on the cheek, turned around and jogged to his car, waving as he drove off.

That's *it?*

She rolled her eyes, disappointed in herself for wanting more. Yet she was relieved that nothing more had happened.

Wasn't she?

Chapter Six

Mari woke up at ten o'clock, unable to remember the last time she'd slept so late.

She hopped in the shower, dressed in sweats and walked over to the patio with her coffee. Sipping the warm brew, she spotted a heron standing on its long, thin legs at the edge of the lake, surrounded by mist. Its pointed beak stabbed at something in the water.

She watched in fascination, wondering if she had the skill to paint it onto one of her pieces.

Quietly, she walked onto the porch, found some

paper and sketched the bird, getting the result she wanted with her fifth attempt.

Excited, she decided to make a couple of dishes on the wheel. She'd paint the heron on a flat surface first.

Just as she picked up a bag of clay, she heard a car coming down the road.

It had to be Brian coming to fix the window.

Her heart raced. Then she felt torn. She had to admit that she liked his company, yet it was a perfect day to be alone, to lose herself in her art.

But he'd said that he wouldn't be long. She went to the porch door and waited for him.

Wearing a perfectly tailored suit, he went into the boathouse and came out carrying a ladder. Wasn't he going to change?

"Good morning," she said, opening the porch door.

He grinned. "Foggy morning, you mean. Too bad you're not getting some sun today."

"I love it." She took a deep breath. "Doesn't it smell good?"

He imitated her intake of breath. "It smells like fish."

"There you go again." She shook her head. "It does *not* smell like fish. It smells like...the lake."

"And where do fish live?" He raised an eyebrow. "I rest my case."

"You are impossible." In spite of his comments, she had to grin. "Are you going to fix the shutter looking like you're going to ring the opening bell at the New York Stock Exchange?"

"I didn't bring extra clothes, and I have some calls to make at the garage today. Later, I'm closing a deal for Jack in Lake George, where I'm going to wrap up another deal on a rare 1908 Tulip Cadillac for Melanie this afternoon in Glens Falls."

"What are Melanie and Jack doing this fabulous misty morning, that you have to pinch hit?"

"Jack is flying to Talladega to hang out with some racing friends. Melanie is speaking to Kyle's class this afternoon about what she does as an antique car restorer. Apparently, it's Career Day for second-graders. That leaves me to pick up the slack." He shrugged.

"Do you always pick up the slack?"

"Of course. They're my family."

It seemed like they stared at each other for minutes, hours. Then Brian turned away.

"Well," he said. "I'd better fix the shutter and get out of your hair."

"Would you like some coffee?"

"I'd love some if it wouldn't be any trouble."

"No trouble. It's all ready." She looked down at his perfectly polished dress shoes. "I hate to be a mother hen, but those don't look like the best shoes for walking on a roof. Won't you slip? It's pretty damp up there."

"I'll be careful." He took off his suit coat and handed it to her.

Men. Could they be any more hardheaded?

He began to climb the ladder in business attire— burgundy tie, pressed white shirt with a "BH" monogram on the pocket. Only Brian would have a monogrammed shirt.

Mari went inside and poured him a cup of coffee and refilled her own. She put milk in a creamer, refilled the sugar bowl and put it all on a tray she'd found in a cupboard. Then she put some cookies she'd bought at Clancy's on another plate.

She heard footsteps on the roof. Brian must be okay still.

Grabbing a roll of paper towels, she carried the tray to the patio and wiped down the furniture so his expensive suit wouldn't get wet.

Brian walked toward her, ladder in hand.

"All set." He set the ladder down and took a seat next to her.

She set down a mug of steaming coffee in front

of him and pushed the tray toward him so he could fix it the way he wanted.

They sat in uneasy silence for a while, then Mari turned toward him. "Can I ask you something?"

"Fire away."

"Why did you choose to go into your family's business?"

"The garage?" He shrugged. "I just grew up there. Whenever I was around, I gravitated to keeping the books, ordering supplies, running the business end. Melanie's creative, so she found her niche with the antique cars. And Jack has the need for speed and glamour, so it was natural that he fell into all things racing."

"But you weren't *expected* to go into the business?"

He shook his head. "Dad never pushed the garage on any of us. He was happy that I went for my MBA. And when I was doing really well at my brokerage firm, he knew I didn't plan on returning to Hawk's Lake." He took a sip of coffee. "What about you? Did you feel like you had a duty to go into Sherwood Enterprises?"

She thought for a while. "Not exactly. Ever since I was a kid, I couldn't wait to work there. It was a way to be near my parents. They were always so focused on the business, I felt like if I was part of that they'd have to focus on me, too."

What on earth was she doing? She'd never admitted that to anyone, and here she was baring her soul.

"And now?"

His beautiful eyes were completely focused on her. He seemed truly interested and tuned in, so she continued.

"And now…I don't know what to do. I just know I need a break from the place."

Brian whistled. "I don't think I wanted or needed a vacation in the five years I worked on Wall Street. I loved the hustle. It was a rush."

"So why didn't you go back? I mean, you said that your family needed you, but why are you still here?"

"First, there was an IRS audit. Then there were two additions to the garage that I wanted to supervise—Dad's not good at that kind of thing. In between everything, Melanie became pregnant, and, as you know, her husband died and I helped out with her son, Kyle. And on it went."

"Whoa…did you say that you *wanted* to supervise the two additions to the garage?"

"Did I say that?" he asked, eyes wide. "I should have said that I *had to* supervise."

"Maybe you like being the go-to guy."

Brian looked at her with eyebrows raised.

"Or maybe it's just family responsibility," Mari said, giving him a way out, but remembering to table this topic for later. "I told my parents that I needed a two-month vacation, but there's more to it than that."

"I'm listening."

"We're going to divide the company. My parents are going to be joint CEOs of new acquisitions and licensing. I'd get all the rest and become CEO. But I need to figure out if I want the job or not."

"It's a wonderful opportunity for you."

"I'm not sure that I want to do it. It's a ton of work. I take work home. I work on the weekends. I never have time for a personal life. Even the men that I've dated were those that worked at Sherwood. Our dates were more like meetings than dates."

She tried to laugh at her joke, but it came out more like a grunt.

"Do you like the work?"

"I used to. I still should. I guess it's just too much now, too big." She sighed. "But I have to work there. It's my family's company."

"That doesn't really answer my question."

"I guess not." She met his gaze and saw concern

in his eyes and in the lines creasing his forehead. "To be honest, at this point, Brian, I don't really know if I like it anymore."

What he wouldn't give for a job like the one being offered to her, thought Brian. CEO of Sherwood Enterprises.

Right now things were calm, and he could go for it if he really wanted. Melanie was deliriously happy with her new husband, busy with her children and the restoration business. Jack had cut back on his races and was spending more time at the garage developing faster race cars. Ed was retired, but at the garage more than ever. And Brian had no problem leaving his real-estate office in the hands of his agents and Mrs. Newley.

Maybe he could keep the books long-distance. Or hire a full-time office manager who would at least enter things on the computer. He could keep up with the other stuff he did for the garage in his spare time.

Deep down, Brian was afraid that if he didn't leave Hawk's Lake now he never would. So, what was he waiting for?

As one professional to another, maybe he should ask Mari to help him.

Though his credentials weren't quite as broad as they probably ought to be, he still figured he had a really good shot at getting the CEO job when—if— Mari decided for sure that she didn't want to take it. Plus, her parents already knew him and had always liked him, and so did Mari for that matter. With a recommendation from her, he'd be a strong candidate.

He was just about to ask Mari, but she was looking off in the distance, as if she were a million miles away.

He took a sip of coffee. "Would you like to row out on the lake with me and look at the stars?" He laughed. "Sorry, that sounds like a bad pick-up line."

She looked at him in surprise. "I—I don't think—"

"Come on, Mari. Get the most out of your Hawk's Lake experience."

"Okay. I'd like that."

"Great." He downed most of his coffee, helped himself to a cookie and waved goodbye. "I've got to hit the road. Busy day today."

"Oh. Your jacket." Hurrying into the cottage, she retrieved it and handed it to him. She gave him a slight smile, but her shoulders slumped as if she'd gone back to carrying a heavy weight on them.

Damn. He thought he might have helped her by letting her talk things out and by answering her questions. Instead, he'd made things worse.

"I'll see you in a couple of days," he said. Then he added, "And if you need to talk some more, I'll listen."

She looked at him. "Really?"

"Of course," Brian answered, holding her gaze. "That's what friends are for."

Brian had spent the last forty-eight hours looking forward to seeing Mari again. And every second of the wait had been worth it. Hawk's Lake glimmered in the moonlight as the crickets chirped around them. The stars shone brilliantly in the dark sky, and Mari seemed relaxed and happy.

"Bri, I want to row. Change places with me," she said.

They stood and the rowboat rocked precariously. He reached out to steady her, his hands on her waist. She slammed into him and clamped on to his T-shirt with her hands.

Their gazes held for a while, and Brian was just about to bend his head and taste her lips when Mari cleared her throat.

"I shouldn't have stood up that fast," she said, her voice a little husky.

He couldn't think of a clever reply—he was still concentrating on her lips.

She slid onto the wooden seat and he took the one opposite, sitting so he faced her. Mari began to row, heading for the middle of the lake. After a few misses with the oars, she made some adjustments and soon they were gliding across the water with barely a ripple.

"Now this is heaven," he joked, stretching his legs out and crossing them at the ankles. "A beautiful woman rowing me around."

She skimmed an oar on the water and tried to splash him. On the third try, she got it right.

"Yeow! That water is cold."

She laughed. "You know you had that coming."

"I suppose so." Her laughter—and her glowing smile—suddenly reminded him of the summer he'd fondly referred to as the year of her pink bikini, when he'd realized that Mari was turning into a woman.

Then there was the year of the kiss, when she was sixteen and he was heading to NYU. The year he didn't—couldn't—say goodbye to her.

"Mari, there's something I want to clear up between us." He took a deep breath. "I've thought about you a lot since that last summer at Hawk's Lake."

The way she bit down on her bottom lip told

him that she didn't believe him. "Then why didn't you ever call?"

"I don't know." He ran a hand through his hair. "I guess the more time that went by, the harder it became."

"I was so mad at you." She met his gaze. "Actually, I was mad at everyone and everything. Sixteen wasn't a fun age for me. My whole world was changing, and way too fast. And my best friend never said goodbye."

"Dammit, Mari. You were only sixteen. I was eighteen. If you want the truth, I was…scared."

"Scared? Why?"

He tried to find the words. "I was scared of my feelings for you. And you were younger than I was. You were sixteen and I was eighteen. That was a big gap back then." He shook his head. "You were going back to Boston—for good. What did I have to offer you? I had a scholarship waiting for me. You had your world—your society events, your family business."

"But you were my best friend, Brian."

He could hear the hurt in her voice.

"And you were mine. That's why I had to let you go—to live your life."

She turned away, and he could see her wiping at her eyes.

"I can't believe how this still hurts me after

twelve long years." She turned and looked at him for what seemed like an eternity. "But I guess I do understand. You meant well."

"Thanks, Mari."

Everything was quiet. He could only hear the swishing sound of the oars pushing through the water. He couldn't take his eyes off Mari. Illuminated by the moonlight, she seemed ethereal, angelic. She was finally back in Hawk's Lake. This time, he didn't want to stay away from her. "Look at all the stars."

She was silent for a while. "You're right, Brian," she whispered. "It seems as though I can reach out and touch them."

Her head was bent back, and he wanted to touch his lips to the curve of her neck.

"I brought some wine," he said. "Are you in?"

"Definitely."

He pulled out a corkscrew from his pocket and, by the glow of a flashlight, he uncorked the wine and poured it into two plastic cups.

"A toast?" he said, holding up his cup.

Mari held up hers, too. "To Hawk's Lake," she said. "The best place in the world."

He had the urge to sit beside her, put his arm around her and let her rest her head on his shoulder, but he didn't want her to move away.

"I know you don't think so, Brian. But that's because you've always lived here. You take things for granted."

She was quiet for a minute. "I'd like to stay here forever."

"Forever is a long time in a place like this. What would you do?"

"Honestly?" She raised an eyebrow, and he nodded. "I would really like to make pottery and sell it in the little gift shops here, and then—" She stopped abruptly. "Well, there's no sense carrying on. I'll probably have to go back."

"So you've thought about it?"

"I never really stop thinking about it, but I don't want to talk about Sherwood. Not on such a beautiful night. But thanks for asking."

She reached over and took his hand, and he took that opportunity to move next to her.

He put his arm around her and hugged her to his side, just like an old friend.

But when he smelled the hint of strawberries on her hair and caught the floral scent of her skin, it was hard to remember that they were just old friends. Or that he'd thrown away any chance for something more.

To distract himself from the ache of wanting her,

he pointed out a couple of constellations, and they sat quietly for a long time, swaying with the motion of the boat and sipping their wine.

When she looked up at him with her sweet smile, he couldn't keep himself from lifting her chin and kissing her. Giving her enough time to protest, he kissed her forehead. When her smile deepened, he touched his lips to hers.

Her arms went around his neck, and she kissed him back. He heard a slight sound of pleasure and he traced her lips with his tongue.

"Mmm…Brian?"

He couldn't get enough of her. She was the one woman he could never get out of his mind.

He realized now he'd been subconsciously comparing all the other women he'd dated to Mari. And they'd never measured up. Never given him that feeling of finding "home" in their arms, as she had—and as she did now.

He felt a push on his arms, and a greater rocking of the boat. He broke the kiss.

"Mari?"

"Brian, what are we doing?" Her eyes were wide with shock.

"Kissing." He grinned.

"We can't be kissing."

"I'm pretty sure that's what we were doing."

She seemed a little tense and gave a nervous laugh, but she cupped her hand over the water, ready to splash him again.

"Okay…okay…maybe I do deserve that," he said. "But you have to admit that you kissed me back."

She let the water drain between her fingers. "It's not you. It's me. I want us to stay friends and not complicate things. And I've made some poor decisions where men are concerned."

He sat straighter. "You think I'm a poor decision?"

"You know what I mean, Bri."

"Okay." He moved back to his seat and picked up the oars. "Do you want to limit our relationship to strictly business?"

"A business relationship? What do you mean by that?" Her eyes narrowed.

"Uh…" What *did* he mean by that? He couldn't just come out and tell her that he wanted her job, could he? Not now. Not when she was so conflicted about whether or not she wanted it herself. "Mari, I know you're afraid of being hurt, but I swear, that's not my intention. I'm not like all those other guys."

He looked out into the darkness. Maybe he was just like them. Maybe he was worse. After all, they only wanted a promotion, but he wanted *her* job.

But as far as their relationship was concerned, his intentions were real. But how could he prove that to her?

Mari sighed. "Give me time, Brian. I need to figure some things out."

He nodded. "Fair enough."

Time was his old enemy. Time had taken Mari away from him every summer, had kept them apart for years.

But not now. Not this time.

Chapter Seven

Mari sat on the big leather side chair in the corner of the great room, with her journal on her lap and a pen in her hand.

She couldn't be any more confused if this day had been her first day of high school.

Doodling on a clean page, she couldn't stop thinking about Brian and the kiss they'd shared under the stars. She could still feel the warmth of his lips on hers, the gentle sway of the rowboat, the press of his body against her own....

She closed her eyes. There were too many pent-up feelings between them. A kiss would surely lead to more. Could she handle a relationship with Brian?

It didn't take a crystal ball to figure out that she could easily fall for him.

Her big crush on him when she was sixteen had been so painful that she'd never thought she'd recover. It seemed that one moment they were kissing, and the next he'd just walked away, out of her life.

And now he was back. She hadn't been able to get him out of her mind since she saw him at the real-estate office the day she arrived. She tried to keep him just as an old friend—but she was beginning to feel more and want more.

They had a history together, but did they have a future together?

After he'd kissed her in the rowboat, it took all the willpower she could muster to push him away. But they were two mature adults. Maybe if they just had a fling, she could get him out of her system. Maybe it would be the best thing that ever happened to her.

Or maybe it would make things worse.

Suddenly, the kitchen phone rang, slicing through the silence. She closed her journal and tried to keep her heart from jumping out of her chest as she hurried to the phone.

"Hello?"

"Mari, it's Brian. I'm on my way back to Sherwood Lodge. If you don't mind, I need to borrow your van. There's been an accident."

She wanted to ask him more questions, but her mouth suddenly went dry.

"I didn't want to scare you," he continued quickly. "That's why I called."

"Are you okay? Can I help?" she asked, finding her voice and reaching for her purse and coat.

"I'm fine. I'm pulling in now."

She ran out the door, down the steps and to the van. Brian was running toward it. She hit the buttons on her key chain to open the locks and tossed the keys to him. "You know where you're going. You drive."

Inside the van, she shrugged into her coat. "What's going on?" Soon they were bouncing down the road.

"I got beeped by Sam."

Mari gasped. "Is Mel okay? Are the kids okay?"

"They're all fine," he assured her. "It's nothing like that. And no one's really hurt, as far as I know. Sam's the director of emergency services for the area. He said that a tour bus of senior citizens ran off the road on Route 28. They'd stopped for dinner and were headed back to Utica. The driver overcorrected when a couple of deer ran into the road. He veered into a ditch, and the bus is now wedged against a rock wall. We need to unload the passengers from the emergency exit in the back of the bus. Medics are on the scene. So are other volunteers. The state police are on the way."

"I'll do whatever I can," Mari said. "Are you a fireman? An EMT?"

"Volunteer fireman. We don't have a full-time fire department."

It didn't surprise her in the least. From his early Boy Scout days, when he rose to the rank of Eagle Scout, Brian had always chosen projects that involved helping others. And his loyalty and responsibility to his family were staggering.

"We only have one ambulance," he explained. "I thought of your van, with its lift, because some of the seniors are in wheelchairs or have impaired mobility."

In her rush to help, she never thought of why Brian was asking to use her van. "Excellent idea."

It was dark and misty, and she was glad that Brian was a skillful driver and knew each curve of the road. Mari could see deer on both sides in the glow of the headlights, and she held her breath that the graceful creatures wouldn't run across their path.

As they turned the next bend, red emergency lights and bright flares came into view. Two firemen were directing traffic. Brian slowed down and rolled down the window. A man with a fluffy black mustache and beard leaned over and peered into the car.

"Hi, Brian."

"Hey, Alex. Everything going okay?"

"Yup. We're unloading the seniors now from the back of the bus. They're being relocated to the summer trolley shuttle for triage. Doc Weatherby and the medics are checking them. Another bus is on the way."

"Where's Sam?" Brian asked.

"He's at the bus with his bullhorn, directing the operation as usual." Rick signaled another car to move on.

"Did Sam tell Melanie to bring the big tow to hook the bus?"

"She's on her way."

Brian nodded. "Where can I park? Give me a spot nearby, in case we need to use this van for transport."

"Park in front of the Pine Cone Restaurant." The fireman blew his whistle and motioned for Brian to go through.

Brian drove very slowly past the accident scene on their left. Mari could see the bus leaning on its side against a wall of rock, just as Brian had said.

Glass sparkled on the road like chips of ice, and she hoped that none of the occupants had been hurt by flying shards.

As they passed the big silver bus, she noticed the passengers being unloaded from the emergency door in the rear. There were many volunteers, and more were pulling into the parking lot of the Pine Cone Restaurant and running to assist.

Brian parked the van on the side of the road at the edge of the lot opposite the bus, near the trolley. "Let's go."

He took her elbow and headed for Sam, who was fielding questions, pointing and directing people.

Sam nodded to both of them as they approached. "There are no real serious injuries from what we can tell, but a lot of bumps and bruises. Some cuts."

"Good. Where do you need us?" Brian asked.

"Brian, you help unload the bus."

"You got it." He turned to Mari. "See you later."

"Okay." Mari watched Brian jog off with an easy gait. His long legs made short work of getting to the bus, and she couldn't help noticing the way his jeans hugged his rear.

"Mari?"

Sam's voice broke through her fogged senses, and she was glad that it was dark so that Sam couldn't see the heat on her cheeks.

"There are blankets in the white utility truck over there." She looked in the direction where he pointed.

"Please pass them out to the people on the trolley. It's getting colder and foggier out here. A replacement bus is on the way, but see what else you can do to make everyone comfortable. The Pine Cone Restaurant is making coffee. Maybe you can help pass that out, too."

"Will do," Marie said, jogging to the white truck. She opened the back end of the vehicle and found several stacks of what looked like green wool army blankets heaped on the shelves. Climbing into the truck, she pulled down two stacks and carried them toward the trolley.

The trolley had open sides, and consisted of about thirty rows of wooden benches. It had a roof and was hooked to a big pickup truck.

She got right to work, passing out blankets and making several trips for more. As volunteers arrived, she sent them for blankets and gave them instructions. Most of the seniors were taking the accident in stride, making it seem like a big adventure. Some were complaining of the cold. She tucked more blankets around them.

She caught glimpses of Brian as he helped the men and women off the bus. Those who seemed to be the most fragile, or the most upset, he escorted himself to the trolley and handed them over to her.

Mari noticed that Brian had the unique ability to joke, tease, calm or comfort depending on the personality of whoever he was with.

The bus was finally empty, and Melanie was backing up the huge Hawkins's Garage tow truck. Jack and Brian sprang into action. They made hand signals to Melanie and did something with chains and hooks. Mari could tell that they'd grown up around a garage—they didn't waste a motion, and knew exactly what they were doing.

Somehow, with all the volunteers and professionals, chains and cables, the bus was righted.

The bus driver drove it to the Pine Cone and parked it while the trolley full of former passengers cheered and clapped.

At one point, Brian sought her out and wrapped his arm around her waist, pulling her to him. "Great job, Mari," he whispered into her ear. "Thanks for coming out to help."

She felt flush with pleasure at his words, but then she centered herself. She was only passing out blankets and coffee, not saving lives on a battlefield. But she liked the compliment anyway. Then someone called her name, and she had to leave Brian to go back to work.

When she turned back, he was grinning at her,

and right now she couldn't think of anyplace she'd rather be, or any person she'd rather be with, than in Hawk's Lake with Brian.

Maybe that meant a fling with Brian wouldn't be such a bad idea after all....

The replacement bus pulled up and the travelers filed on. They'd been lucky—no one needed to go to the hospital. Brian watched as Mari got many hugs and gracious thanks from the passengers.

They went into the Pine Cone where the owners had set out several pizzas, coffee and pitchers of soda and beer. It was a cozy place, with wood benches for chairs and rectangular tables with forest-green tablecloths. The walls were covered in yellowed knotty pine planks and decorated with pictures of the various peaks of the Adirondacks.

Brian took the opportunity to introduce Mari to everyone present. Several remembered her family, and she was welcomed back many times.

Brian finally guided her to a table where Jack, Melanie and Sam were already sitting.

"Whew! What a night," Mari said, taking a chair. "You know what I love the most about Hawk's Lake?"

"The pizza?" Jack handed her a piece on a paper plate.

"That, too." She laughed. "But I just love the way everyone here pulls together."

"And everyone knows your business," Brian added.

They all laughed, but Brian noticed that Mari didn't join in. He realized his constant criticism of Hawk's Lake was upsetting her, which he supposed made sense, given that she felt more alive and at home here than anywhere else.

Gus Belden stopped by the table, clamped a meaty hand on Brian's shoulder and squeezed. "Great job, everyone." He nodded to Mari. "Thanks for pitching in."

Brian introduced Mari to Gus. "We went to high school together. Gus owns a bait and tackle shop in Big Moose."

"Pleased to meet you," Mari said, holding out her hand.

Gus shook it and turned his attention back to Brian. "Bri, Matt Logan was just telling us that his son Josh has to have an operation for his tumor— it's in his lung. They boy's doctor wants to send him to St. Jude's."

"But I just saw Matt here tonight. He was helping me evacuate the bus," Brian said.

Gus puffed out his cheeks and shook his head. "You know Matt. He'll always help. But the guy doesn't have any insurance since he lost his job when the lumberyard in Big Moose closed."

"And we'll help *him*." Brian pulled a pen from his pocket and started making notes on a paper napkin. "I'm thinking the fire hall. We'll get some donations for a silent auction." He made some notes. "And what about a barbecue out back, maybe some small rides for the kids?"

"Brilliant. I knew you'd have some great ideas," Gus said.

"Sherwood Enterprises will donate silverware, glassware and other household items." Mari leaned forward. "I'd love to help."

Brian took her hand. "Thanks, Mari."

Gus took off his baseball cap and crumpled it in his hand. "Thank you, ma'am. That's really nice of you."

"Round up a committee, Gus. We'll meet in my office. Let's aim for this Friday at eight."

"You got it." Gus slapped his hat back on his head and headed for another table.

"What were you just saying, Brian?" Mari asked, scratching her head with her index finger. "Something about how people in Hawk's Lake will help you, whether or not you want it?" She opened her eyes wide and blinked them rapidly several times.

"You know what I mean."

"Do *you* know what you mean?" She blew out air in obvious exasperation. "You try to disown the town, but then you cheerfully walk right back in."

Point well taken, he thought. But he wasn't about to admit that she might be right. That would mean that he'd become complacent—that he'd given up his dreams.

And he wasn't ready to give up just yet.

They stayed for a while longer.

Brian checked his watch. "Two in the morning. I think it's time to go home."

They said their goodbyes to everyone on their way out, and were soon driving back to Sherwood Lodge.

"What a night," Brian said.

"It was a great night." She leaned back on the seat. "Makes me feel like I did something to help the community."

"Why do you say that? I know Sherwood contributes a lot to various organizations, and now you're donating to the fund-raiser."

"But that's different. Tonight, I did something...personally."

"But aren't you on several charitable boards?"

"How do you know that?"

"I get your annual report. I'm a stockholder."

"You are?" she asked, definitely surprised.

"It was my high school graduation present. I told my dad that I wanted stock in Sherwood Enterprises."

"That's so cool." She covered her mouth with both hands to hide another yawn.

"You're nodding off. Move closer. I don't want you to bang your head against the window."

"I'm fine."

But to his surprise, she did move closer, and he put his arm around her.

It felt so right being with Mari. And when she rested her head on his shoulder, he could smell the fresh scents of the evening on her hair.

They'd just worked together like two halves of a whole, and he'd really felt a connection to her. It seemed as if there wasn't anything Mari couldn't do.

Except make a decision about their relationship.

He could hear her steady, gentle breathing and felt very protective of her. If there were a way to wrap Mari in a bubble so no harm would ever come to her, or no one would ever hurt her again, he'd do it.

But who would protect Mari from him?

Chapter Eight

For the next few days, Mari couldn't get her mind off of Brian Hawkins.

When she was forming clay on her wheel, she thought of him. Whenever she went on her walks along the shoreline, she rehashed their conversations. And when she tried to read a book, she couldn't concentrate because she wondered what he was doing.

For a change of scenery, she decided to return to Clancy's and get a few odds and ends.

It was a great day—hot and sunny. The scent of pine and cedar hung in the air, and she took a deep breath as she maneuvered the twists and turns of Route 28.

She pulled into a parking spot, stopped to pet a beagle puppy that struggled to reach her from a leash, and exchanged greetings with people she passed.

Inside Clancy's, she checked her list and headed for the paint area to buy some solvent for her paint-brushes—and almost knocked Brian over as she turned the aisle with her cart.

Judging by the surprise on his face, he hadn't expected to see her, either. She remembered how he looked by the light of the moon, how he felt and tasted.

Shaking off the memory, she met his gaze. If she wasn't mistaken, he was studying her, too.

As usual, he was dressed in a suit, but for a change there was no tie. "What is this, casual Friday at the office?" she joked, hoping a little humor would alleviate the tension that hung between them.

"Today's Thursday." He grinned, holding six boxes of business envelopes. "What are you doing here? You were going stir-crazy all alone on the lake, right?"

She wasn't going to admit that he'd guessed cor-rectly, so she just smiled. "I needed some solvent. And coffee."

"We can't go on meeting like this—at Clancy's, of all places." He smiled. "I was just going to grab some lunch. Would you like to join me?"

She wondered if she should, then decided that she couldn't resist his friendly invitation. "I'd love to."

They both cashed out, and she put her purchases on the floor of her van. By the time she walked to his car, he had the top down on his slick black Mustang. She was glad about that. It was the perfect day for riding in a convertible.

They didn't have far to go. He soon pulled into Aunt Betty's Pancake House.

Inside, the restaurant was a huge, barn-shaped place full of birch canoes, old pictures and rusted farm implements hanging from the weathered wood walls. A sign that pictured a moose eating a big salad at a picnic table read, Please sit anywhere.

"I have to show this to you," he said, pointing to an old photo on the wall by a pair of antlers. "It's a picture of Ezra Hawkins, my great-great-grand-father. He founded Hawk's Lake in 1865. This is a picture of his old smithy. It was on the same site as Hawkins's Garage."

She was a little surprised that he wanted to show her his connection to the village, his family's history. Leaning closer, she studied the picture.

"He looks so…distinguished. I can see the family resemblance in this picture."

His hand slipped possessively around her waist as she straightened. She should have stepped away, but it felt so natural, so good.

"It must be amazing being a direct descendant of the founder of this town. This is your history! All this is here because of your ancestors, and your family."

He thought for a moment. "I guess when you put it that way…"

She'd love to find a way to connect him to his own hometown. At least he was thinking now. Maybe what she'd been saying was sinking in. That was a start.

"I just wish that someday you'd realize how much you've done for the village and how much you are appreciated."

"But, Mari—"

"You've also tried to preserve the history of Hawk's Lake. Sherwood Lodge is a perfect example. You even kept the original color scheme." She wanted to take his hand, but she was afraid he'd read it the wrong way.

"I own several historical properties. I believe in preservation."

His blue eyes sparkled at her praise, and she knew he was pleased.

As they walked through the restaurant, every waitress greeted Brian and motioned for him to sit in their area. He picked a spot by the window that overlooked a little waterfall and what must be a trout stream. Fishermen dressed in waders were casting in the water and on the bank of the stream.

Children frolicked in a fenced-in playground to the left as their mothers watched from a bench.

One little boy was crying as his mother comforted him. She rubbed his back with one hand and reached into her purse with her other hand. She wiped off the boy's knee with a tissue that she'd wet with her water bottle, and gently taped on a plastic bandage.

She dabbed at his eyes with another tissue, and soon he was smiling and showing off his new bandage to his playmates.

Mari's chest constricted. She wanted to make her own children smile, to comfort them when they were hurt, to hold their little bodies close to her and shower hugs and kisses on them throughout the day and night.

She wanted to help them with their homework and watch them grow into happy adults with their own families.

Would she ever get that chance?

Reluctantly, Mari pulled herself out of her daydream and brought herself back to the restaurant.

This certainly wasn't one of the fanciest restaurants she'd ever been in, but it definitely had an interesting view.

"I'd love to live here," she blurted without thinking.

Brian leaned back in his chair. "Wow. That was quite the announcement. We didn't even order yet. But you aren't telling me anything that you haven't said before."

She glanced out the window. "Look outside, Brian. Tell me what you see."

He followed her line of vision. "I see guys fishing. Kids at the playground. Just the usual spring activities, after everyone thaws out after winter."

She'd give anything to be one of those mothers watching her children playing on the playground. Hawk's Lake would be a perfect place to raise a family.

One of the men was reeling in a fish as the others watched. She could just picture Brian standing on the riverbank, patiently showing their children how to fish.

Their children? Her face heated. Okay, she had to admit that, lately, he'd been on her mind, too—but this was carrying her dreams a bit too far.

She might want to sleep with him, but another engagement? Marriage? She'd been burned too many times to even add that to her ever-growing list of things to think about.

"What do *you* see, Mari?" he asked.

"I see families together, taking time out to enjoy life. Fresh air. Nature."

"Okay." He shrugged.

"You just don't get it, Brian," she snapped, trying to get her emotions under control. "For example, Aunt Betty offers pancakes, but she also serves everything else you can think of. And look at these prices. They're so low, it's unbelievable."

"They'll raise the prices in the summer, when the tourists hit. You can be sure of that. And Aunt Betty is really an ex-sailor by the name of Melvin Ray. Those fishermen on the river there are probably avoiding their wives, and those ladies on the bench at the playground are gossiping and avoiding their husbands."

Her blood began to boil. "Just stop. Why do you have to be so cynical?"

"You're romanticizing Hawk's Lake. I'm just pointing out what's wrong with it."

"Well, don't do that anymore. Okay?"

"If that's what you want."

The waitress came and Mari was glad for the interruption. She just couldn't understand Brian's thinking. He had the best of everything right here.

Obviously, the two of them didn't want the same things.

Her throat tightened, and she didn't think that she could swallow the chicken-salad sandwich that she'd planned on ordering.

Glancing at the menu again, she ordered chicken soup instead. Brian got a burger with the works and some fries. The waitress didn't seem in a hurry to leave their table, and kept smiling at Brian, checking several times as to how he wanted his burger cooked. She was obviously attracted to him.

Who wouldn't be?

Mari remembered being fascinated with him, too, as they rowed on the lake under the stars and worked together at the scene of the accident. However, right now at Aunt Betty's Pancake House, she wished she could get Brian to see Hawk's Lake through her eyes.

But why was that so important to her?

"What attracts you to cities?" she asked, coming at it from another direction. "Granted, cities are fabulous, but they're tough places to raise a family."

He shrugged. "I had the best time when I was living in New York with three other guys. We worked long hours—days, nights, weekends—and somehow we still partied and had a great time. When the boss needed us at any time of the day or night, we were there. And the money was incredible."

"So was your rent, I'm sure. I'll bet you had to live four in an apartment to make the monthly rent. And I'll bet it was a dump, and on the top floor, without an elevator. But you were young and just out of college, so you didn't care. And just how long do you think you could've kept up that pace?"

"Who knows?" He shrugged. "But it was the best time of my life."

"Why isn't *now* the best time of your life?"

"Time flies, Mari. And I have a lot of unfinished plans."

Lunch came and it was just as well. Their discussion was getting too heated.

They discussed lighter topics after their food was served, and even lingered over pie and coffee. Mari couldn't remember the last time she'd had a long, leisurely lunch. Usually, she had Julie order her something from the basement cafeteria or from a local deli and had it delivered to her office. More often than not, she skipped the meal altogether.

This was a much nicer way to spend her lunchtime, even if they had to agree to disagree.

* * *

"I have a meeting at four at the village hall, but if you'd like, there's still time to sit on one of the benches by the river for a while and watch the guys fish," Brian said.

"Great idea."

He shed his jacket and tossed it in the backseat of his car. Then they walked to the side of the building.

It was a beautiful day, and he planned on enjoying every second with Mari that he could.

"So you have a meeting to go to?" Mari faked a big shudder. "I hate to even *say* the word *meeting*. It's been great not even thinking of having to attend…those things."

"But this is a fun meeting. We are going to be scheduling the village events for next year and discussing some new ideas."

"What kind of events?"

"The usual ones—the Snow Festival, the Fourth of July fireworks and parade, the craft weekend, the sidewalk art show—things like that." He smiled, thinking of the full calendar.

"I'd like to attend every one of them. And you're smiling, Brian. You love doing things like that."

"I guess I do. It's great to see the village full of

families enjoying themselves. And some of them are fund-raisers for good causes. I've got a couple of great ideas for a couple of new things to try." He felt his blood pumping, excited.

He was starting to sound like Mari about Hawk's Lake.

"Tell me about your ideas."

"An old-fashioned barn dance for Halloween, with games for the kids and their families. And I've been trying to get a big bass fishing tournament here. I got word today that it's a go. That'll bring in a big crowd, and it will benefit everyone. The residents will make money, and the contestants will take back a ton of memories."

"Those are great ideas." Mari put a hand on his arm, and the heat hit him immediately. "I wish you could hear the enthusiasm in your voice. You just love doing things like this—organizing activities and working to bring in tourists and spectators. And that's great for Hawk's Lake."

"And you're not doing what you like at Sherwood, right?"

"We're not talking about me. We're talking about you." She nudged his shoulder with hers. "In spite of how you bash this place, it's your own personal playground."

"I just pitch in. Do what I can. Project the expenses and profits. Whatever."

"Don't be so modest, Brian. I'll bet you do a lot more than you'll admit." She put her hand on his chest, and he thought he was going to melt. "And you do it from your heart."

He was speechless. If Mari was right, it would mean that he was trying to escape a place that he really loved. It would also mean that he'd been dreaming of another job—another life—when he already had everything he'd been working for.

Damn.

Chapter Nine

Mari slowly spun the clay on her wheel. This was the critical time, when she was going to pull up the side of the bowl, and she wanted it to be as even as possible.

She heard the crunch of footsteps on gravel, saw Brian's reflection in the side window. "Come in," she yelled. "I can't open the door right now."

He stood behind her, and his special scent of pine and spice drifted over her.

"I'll be right with you." The bowl did exactly what she wanted it to. Perfect.

She looked up at Brian. He seemed to be mesmerized. She lifted her foot and the wheel stopped. She found her wire and carefully cut the bowl from the remaining clay.

"Hello." Just looking at him signaled the butterflies in her stomach to start fluttering. He was wearing faded jeans that were a perfect fit, along with a black T-shirt. His sneakers were barely scuffed.

"What brings you here?" she asked.

"I wanted to paint and caulk a couple of window frames that I noticed needed some work. I won't bother you."

His mere presence would bother her, in more ways than one.

Brian looked around at the completed pieces. "This is beautiful work." He walked around the porch and looked at her finished pottery. "May I pick it up?"

"Sure." It pleased her that he was interested. "It's pretty sturdy."

"I love this heron that you painted. And the ducks in the cattails are wonderful. And the colors and sheen. What's it called?"

"Glaze. My grandmother taught me how to mix and what to add for the best results." She winked. "I'd tell you my recipe, but it's a family secret."

"I wouldn't know what to do with it, anyway."

She smiled. "Would you like something for yourself?"

"I'd love this heron mug. Or maybe the one with the ducks."

She took them both off the shelf and handed them to him. "Take them both." Their fingers brushed, and she got some clay on his. "I'm sorry." She found a clean rag and brushed the dirt from his hands.

"Let me wash up," Mari said, "and I'll show you something in the boathouse. It's my favorite thing. Do you have time?"

"I do."

From the sink in the kitchen, she could see him walk around and examine more of her pieces. Moments later, she joined him on the porch and they walked to the boathouse, where her kiln was stationed. She unlocked the latches and pulled up the lid. "Now look."

They both peered into the six-sided barrel. "Isn't it amazing—all the colors?" she asked, hoping that he'd think so, too.

Brian let out a long whistle. "I can see why you think that this is the best part."

She pulled out piece after piece—different colors, the same colors, experimental shapes and sizes.

Brian helped her load everything into a cushioned wheelbarrow.

"Mari, if you're interested in selling your pottery, I can think of several gift shops in the area that would love to carry it."

Her heart beat faster. "Really?"

"Absolutely."

"That's just how Great-Great-Grandma Violet Sherwood got started. Well, mostly." Mari chuckled. "She had a carriage house, I have a boathouse."

"I happen to have some boxes in my car. We'll pack up whatever you want to sell, and I'll make some calls at the gift shops in town. Or maybe you'd like to handle it yourself."

Mari shook her head. "I'll pick out some pieces, but if you don't mind, I'd appreciate it if you would do it." She didn't know if she could handle rejection—not of something so personal as her art. Besides, he knew everybody.

That was a new feeling. She didn't care when a store chose not to carry Sherwood Enterprises products or rejected certain collections. She just had her sales staff move on.

Sherwood was her family legacy, just as Brian had pointed out. But her pottery was *hers*. It was something that she'd always longed to do, but had never made time for.

Without Sherwood, she had the time. Her life could be hers to live as she chose, and luckily, she had saved enough money to last several lifetimes.

Then what was so hard about making a decision?

Brian was a good sounding board, and he was easy to talk to. He also knew her family background, her history.

Mari took a deep breath. She enjoyed Brian's company and his sense of humor. He was dependable and caring, that was evident when he returned home to be with his family when they needed him. He had yet to realize how much Hawk's Lake actually meant to him, but she was trying to help him with that.

And undoubtedly, she was definitely physically attracted to him, and she knew that the feeling was mutual.

There was nothing wrong with a few kisses—or more—to satisfy their desire.

She'd love to trust her old friend, but to do that would take a leap of faith, and Mari didn't know if she had that kind of trust in her anymore. She'd trusted one too many times, and a person could only take so much hurt—so much betrayal. Sometimes it felt as if she didn't have it in herself to believe one more time that someone could love her just for herself.

Up on his ladder against the wall of Sherwood Lodge, Brian worked on a couple of windows, digging out old caulk and applying the new. When done, he looked around at the landscape.

It was turning into an unseasonably hot afternoon, which was good. It'd dry up the lawn and tweak the wildflowers into blooming sooner. He had to admit that, after a long winter, he liked seeing all the flowers.

Knowing Mari, she'd like that, too. She always used to pick wildflowers and bring them back to Sherwood Lodge for the kitchen table.

He unscrewed one of the shutters on Mari's front bedroom window. He might as well paint them, too. He couldn't help but look into the room as he did it, and noticed that the bed was perfectly made up. There was a book open on the desk right beneath the window.

"Brian?"

The shutter dropped out of his hands, slid down the roof, hit the ladder a few times and rested on the grass. If it didn't need painting before, it did now.

"Oh, sorry. I didn't mean to disturb you," Mari said, looking up from the ground. "I just wanted to know if you needed anything."

"You know, Mari, it's such a nice day. Want to row over to Secret Island?" he asked. "We could have a picnic."

"Secret Island? But what about mean Mr. Yeller—you know, the guy who always shooed us away?"

"I bought the island from him."

"You did?" She grinned. "When we were kids, you always said that you were going to own it one day."

"I thought it'd be a good investment."

The truth was, he couldn't stand the thought of someone else making memories on *their* secret island.

She shaded her eyes and looked west toward the slice of land floating in Hawk's Lake. The tip of it stuck out like a finger.

It seemed like she was contemplating whether she should go or not.

"Oh, Brian! Let's go!"

"Good," he said, glad that he'd made her happy and eager to show her the island.

"I'll pack us some things to eat."

"Okay. I'll drive over to Hawk's Roost and get the speedboat. I'll pick you up at the dock here."

"Great." She turned to leave.

"Oh, Mari?"

She stopped. "Yes?"

"Bring a bathing suit."

"You can't be serious. It'll be freezing."

"Trust me."

He watched as she hurried to the cottage, a happy bounce to her step.

Picking up his pace, he hurried to his car. He'd take care of the shutters another time. Right now, he had better things to do.

Mari couldn't believe how great it felt to skim across crystal-clear Hawk's Lake in a lemon-yellow boat. It was a sleek, shiny craft that would be perfect for waterskiing.

Her hair flew around in the wind, and she let her hand catch the spray from the wake of the boat.

She looked at Brian standing behind the wheel. He was concentrating on the water straight ahead, even though there wasn't a soul on the lake. The sun made his face and hands look almost ruddy, as if he spent his days outdoors. She liked this casual Brian as much as she liked him in a suit.

"Remember when we used to paddle our canoes out here? It took us all day," she said. "But we were explorers discovering a new world. And whenever we were just about to set foot on Mr. Yeller's island, he would appear."

"He once told me that, in retrospect, he should have just invited us over, and we could have gotten it out of our system." Brian laughed. "Then it wouldn't have held such mystery."

He skillfully pulled up to the dock and cut the motor. In one swift motion, he was out of the boat and tying it up.

"I would have helped," Mari said.

"I got it." He held his hand out, and she handed him a tote bag and a backpack. Then she held out her hand to him. "Step on the seat cushion. I got you."

His grip was strong, and he made sure that she was steady. He slipped his arm around her waist, and they walked down the dock. It felt natural, as if they'd walked like this a million times, but he knew different. He was waiting for her to pull away from him soon.

She was swaying a little, but it subsided. "I'm okay now." Looking up at a log structure mostly hidden by trees, she smiled. "Who's living there?"

"No one." She was still in his arms, and he liked how they fit together like two puzzle pieces. "I rent it out during the summer. The same family comes back year after year."

"Can I see the house?" she asked.

"Sure. That's where we're going."

Surrounded by pines, Canadian hemlocks and white and yellow trilliums that were in bloom, they walked up a worn path strewn with rusty-colored pine needles to the cabin.

Mari stopped and looked at the simple structure. "It's much bigger than I'd thought."

"Wait until you see the inside," Brian said, lifting several large rocks until he found a key. "And the gazebo."

He opened the door and they went in. Mari stood in the middle of the place, her mouth gaping in awe. It was rustic and grand at the same time. Knotty pine planks covered the walls. Brightly striped Hudson's Bay blankets and authentic-looking Adirondack pack baskets hung from the rafters. Log furniture was positioned around a floor-to-ceiling river-rock fireplace. The mantel looked like a slab of pink granite. A stone stairway led upstairs to a loft where more striped blankets hung like tapestries on a castle wall. A modern kitchen was tucked into a back corner.

"This is just magnificent, Brian."

"I knew you'd like it. Now, prepare to be surprised," he said, taking her hand. He led her to a sunporch. When he opened the big French doors, Mari could see a gazebo made of hewn logs. Stone steps large enough for sitting surrounded a similar stone platform that circled around what looked like a small pool. Brian flipped a switch, and Mari could hear the bubbling of water.

"A hot tub?"

He looked deep into her eyes and gave her hand a squeeze. "Are you interested?"

Her stomach fluttered in nervous excitement. "Yes."

Mari walked back into the house. It didn't take her any time at all to change into her suit. When she walked into the backyard, she noticed Brian's clothes hanging from a tree. He had on a pair of swim shorts that weren't too loose or too tight, but clung in all the right places.

He studied her body, too, and she was glad that she'd bought a new bathing suit. It was a generously cut two-piece and she liked the bright fuchsia color.

He gave a long, low whistle, and she chuckled. That sounded good.

"No pink bikini?" he asked.

"A *what?*"

"I think it might have been the summer when you were fourteen."

"Ah. I remember it now," Mari said.

"Obviously, not at much as I do."

Finally, Mari set her tote bag down on a tall table within reach of the hot tub. "I have wine and some cheese."

"Sounds good." He held out his hand. "Shall we?"

He waited as Mari walked up the stairs and into the tub. Then he joined her.

She sat down and stretched out, letting out a deep breath. Jets bubbled up from everywhere. "I could do laps in this tub, it's so big." She sighed as the warm water relaxed her body. "I can't remember how long it's been since I've done anything like this."

That was a loaded statement.

Brian sat next to her. "Me, either. There's not enough time in the day. But maybe we should make time. Maybe we only *think* we're indispensable."

"You're probably right," Mari said, noticing how the breeze ruffled Brian's hair. "You know, I should have taken more vacations. I wouldn't be so burned out. What about you?"

"I've never been burned out. I went to the stock car races a few times to catch Jack racing, but that was just a couple of overnights—nothing longer than a few days. Tons of people." He sat down lower in the tub. "Not my idea of a vacation."

"But I'll bet the two Hawkins men attracted a lot of women."

He shrugged. "Jack seems to have his share of groupies."

"Oh, I'm sure they swarmed around you, too."

He smiled. "I wouldn't say swarmed, but I've dated my share."

"I'll bet you did."

"How about some wine?" he asked, changing the subject.

She started to get up, but he put a hand on her arm. "Relax, Mari. I'll get it."

He walked up the steps, and Mari noticed that his wet swim trunks were clinging to him, distinctly outlining a well-endowed bulge. She splashed hot water on her face. It did nothing to cool her down. She really should be doing laps in the cold lake.

He returned to the hot tub and Mari tried not to look—but that was like trying not to breathe. He handed her a cup of wine.

"Thanks." She barely croaked out the word.

"A toast," he said, holding up his plastic cup. "To you, Mari. I hope you find what you're looking for."

She held up her cup. "I'll definitely drink to that." She took a sip. "Thanks for this, Brian. You know, I think that Mr. Yeller did have a treasure up here—this hot tub and this incredible location. I'll bet he regrets giving this up."

"He did."

That was shocking, coming from him. "I'm right? Aren't you going to say something like it was a good decision that he finally got out of Hawk's Lake?"

He met her gaze. "You know, Mari, I owe you an apology." He set his cup down, took her hand and looked into her eyes. "I keep trashing Hawk's Lake. I didn't mean to spoil your experience, your reunion with the place. That was inconsiderate of me."

She didn't know how to answer him, but she didn't have to. Without a word, he took the cup from her hand and put it on the edge of the tub next to her. Then he leaned over, slipped his arm around her waist, bent his head toward her and kissed her.

Mari returned the kiss, letting her hands explore his warm, wet chest. She traced a rivulet of water with her index finger as it dripped from a strand of his hair, down his nipple, until it disappeared on the surface of the water. She felt him shiver.

"Forgive me?" he whispered against her lips.

She could barely concentrate on what he was apologizing for. "Yes. Of course."

He watched her every movement, his turquoise

eyes at one with the sky. They seemed to scorch her already warm skin. She could hear his deep intake of air as he pulled her to straddle his lap, where his arousal was obvious.

All she wanted was to feel Brian's hands on her.

She felt his fingers brushing her back and untying the string of her bathing suit top, then the tug of the wet material. His gaze lingered for the longest time as a sexy smile teased his lips.

He tossed the top of her bathing suit on the top step of the tub, and she felt the cool air on her skin—then the warmth of his hands as he cupped her breasts. His thumbs teased her nipples, and a shock of pleasure coursed through her.

With the steam floating around them, she felt like they were in their own little world. On this island, they were.

She reached for the waistband of his bathing suit and slid it down his slim hips. He tucked his fingers under the waistband of her suit bottoms. Then she felt his splayed fingers on her hips, on her buttocks—teasing her.

She couldn't stand it any longer—she had to feel his touch without the confines of the fabric, so she gripped his wrists and helped him take it off.

Stepping out of it, she kicked it to the surface of the water, then added it to the wet pile.

They held each other, legs tangled, steam coming from their bodies as their hearts pounded in unison. He lifted her up, and she wrapped her legs around his waist, feeling the length of him pressing against her.

"Mari?"

She knew what he was asking, and nodded. But he turned away from her.

"I'll be right back."

What?

With a quick vault, he was out of the tub and rummaging through the pockets of his jeans. He yanked out his wallet, flipped it open and pulled out a couple of foil packets.

She'd been so caught up in the moment, she hadn't even thought about protection. Thank goodness Brian remembered.

Instead of sitting in the tub, he stood on the seat and opened the foil packet with his teeth. She could see him—erect and hard—and beautiful to look at.

"Don't move, Brian." She held out her hand to take the packet. "Let me."

She slipped it out of the wrapper. Ever so slowly, she rolled it up his length. Thick and ready, he looked down at her through hooded eyes. He cupped her chin and winked—a hint of things to come.

Then he was in the water, pulling her onto his lap again, so that she was straddling him. He kissed her breasts, taking each nipple into his mouth. His erection rubbed against her core, teasing her, tormenting her.

"Now, Brian. Please. Now," she whispered.

He slowly entered her.

"More. I want more."

He filled her completely and waited. Tracing her jawline with a finger, he gazed into her eyes and began a slow slide, in and out. Picking her up, he moved to the middle of the hot tub, her legs around his waist, and buried himself inside her. The water bubbled around them, their bodies clinging.

She kissed his neck, his forehead. He moved faster, faster still.

"Mari, you feel so good, so tight."

"I knew it'd be like this. Wonderful." Her voice didn't even sound like hers. "Perfect."

He was still holding her to him, his strong arms surrounding her. He was breathing heavy, his eyes closed. She met his every motion. Hard. Harder still.

She felt her release coursing through her body, and Brian soon followed.

When the last wave of pleasure passed, she opened her eyes. Brian was smiling at her. She smiled back. While he was still hard within her, they hugged, content to stay in each other's arms.

No regrets, she reminded herself. All she wanted was to savor this day, this moment, this man.

Chapter Ten

What a day, Mari thought as they pulled into the boathouse at Sherwood Lodge.

She'd wanted a fling with Brian—a brief romance—to get him out of her system. Well, she was well on her way.

A twinge of guilt settled in her gut. She didn't know if she could keep things light with Brian. Even though they'd been apart for a long time, there was still something about him that she…liked.

She didn't want to use the word *love*. That was traveling into dangerous territory—and she didn't want to go there. Not again. Not yet. Maybe never.

It would be less complicated just to be alone, be by herself. Yet even as those thoughts penetrated her mind, her mouth opened and she found herself asking, "Would you like to watch the sun set with me?"

"Sounds good."

They walked hand in hand to the water's edge, and soon got comfortable in lawn chairs.

"This is so nice," Mari said. "So relaxing."

"The next time we do this, we'll need to have another bottle of wine."

"Deal."

Brian put his arm around her shoulder, and they sat in comfortable silence, watching the light show of the setting sun. Listening to the water lap gently against the shore, until he worked up the nerve to break the silence.

"Have you decided to take the CEO job yet?" he asked, a little too eagerly.

She'd been procrastinating about her decision. Why did he have to bring it up now, and bring her back to reality?

"It's been on my mind."

"But no final decision yet?" he asked.

"No."

"What are the pros and cons? Why don't you run them by me?"

A tiny tingle of doubt tickled the back of her neck. Why was he so anxious to hear her answer? As soon as the thought popped into her head, she pushed it away. She needed to learn to trust again, to let down her guard and believe that people cared for her and not her company or what she could do for them. She wanted to believe that the man who sat beside her was that person.

"Let's not talk about it now," she said quietly.

He shrugged. "I was just trying to help."

Maybe Brian was just making conversation, and she was making a big deal out of nothing.

She hoped that was his intention.

Please don't let Brian be like the others.

But it was impossible to trust him. Just like deciding what to do about Sherwood was impossible. And instead of coming to Hawk's Lake to be alone to think and relax, she was making things worse by getting involved with Brian.

"If you don't mind, I'm going to go to bed. I feel a headache coming on," she said.

That was almost the truth.

Stupefied, Brian watched as Mari's slender figure slipped away and disappeared into the gathering dusk. What the hell happened? One minute she seemed fine, the next she developed a headache. And her headache started when he'd asked if she'd made a decision. Then she'd become quiet and guarded.

That harmless little question had obviously made her upset and uncomfortable.

Confused, he picked up the two bags that he'd left on the patio, walked up to the cottage and set them on a chair inside the porch. The house was quiet.

He let himself out and locked the door behind him.

It was then he noticed that he hadn't picked up the shutters. Not knowing when he'd be back, he decided that he'd better put them in the barn.

Maybe he'd head back to his office and catch up on some work.

But he never went to the real-estate office. On his way home, he saw that The White Dove Gift Shop was still open. He parked the car, grabbed the two mugs that Mari had given him and climbed the stairs.

Mari took a bite out of the warm sugar cookie that was cooling on the new rack that she'd bought at Clancy's. She'd made three batches this morning, and they were stacked everywhere. The first batch had burned, so she'd tossed them and started over, being more vigilant with the old oven.

But there was no one to enjoy them with.

She thought of inviting Melanie over for coffee, but she was probably busy with her baby or working at the garage.

She opened the windows, sat down at the kitchen table and looked at the turquoise blue of the glittery lake. Taking a sip of red raspberry tea that she'd bought at Cathy's Tea Cozy, she deliberately tried to concentrate on her beautiful surroundings and not think of Brian or Sherwood Enterprises.

The smell of the cookies filled the air and mingled with the fresh, sun-warmed morning breeze.

The phone rang, startling her as it always did. It was such a foreign sound in the peace and quiet.

She hoped it wasn't Brian. She just didn't want to deal with the whole situation anymore.

"Hello?" she said cautiously.

"How are you doing in the wilderness, dear?"

"I'm terrific, Mother. How is everyone?"

They made small talk for a while, and Mari wondered why her mother had really called.

"Have you met anyone interesting?"

"Do you remember Brian Hawkins?" Just saying his name reminded her of their day together yesterday.

"I do. I always found him to be very studious and polite. He's from a fine family, and if my recollection is correct, he's a descendant of the founder of the town."

Mari smiled without amusement. That made Brian a blue blood in her mother's eyes. As if that was all that mattered.

"What's he doing now?"

"He has a real-estate office and is the business manager for his family's auto shop. He's also a volunteer fireman and a member of the chamber of commerce here. Seems like he has his hands in all kinds of ventures."

And he can do wonderful things with his hands.

Her face heated as she thought of their time in the hot tub. She had to calm down. If her mother even suspected anything was going on between her and a man, she'd be picking out her mother-of-the-bride dress.

"Brian even has stock in Sherwood." Mari took a sip of tea. "He told me that he's had an interest in the company since he's known us, and has followed it throughout the years."

"Sounds like the two of you have reconnected."

If she only knew.

"He sounds like a good catch. Are you two serious?"

Her mother always knew how to cut to what she really wanted to know. But Mari wasn't ready to admit how much Brian meant to her—or how she was still guarding her heart, trying to trust him.

"Nothing serious, Mother. And I realize that I'm not getting any younger and there needs to be more Sherwoods to carry on the legacy."

"Marigold, you know that's not what I meant. I just want to see you happy. That's all your father and I have ever wanted for you."

She helped herself to another cookie and didn't comment on her mother's statement. If they'd wanted her to be happy, then they wouldn't have sold this cottage in the first place. They would have spent more time at home and less at the office.

"I don't need a man to be happy, Mother."

There was another pause. "Have you decided yet if you want to take over as CEO?"

Ah—so this was the *real* reason for her call. Just what Brian had asked her. Did the whole world want to know her answer?

But wait—she'd never told her mother that she had any reservations about taking the job.

Mari was shocked. "H-How did you know? I didn't tell anyone that I—"

"Your father and I figured out it wasn't only the Jason Fox debacle that had you wanting to take a two-month vacation. You haven't been happy for a while. You haven't been yourself."

She'd never expected that her parents had a clue as to what she'd been going through. Why didn't they just ask her? Then again, why didn't she just tell them?

"I don't know if this is the right time, Mother. I was hoping to talk to you and Father together, but since you already suspect, I'm leaning toward not taking the job."

Silence.

"Mother?"

"Will you be returning to the company at all, Marigold? Are you leaving completely?"

She could hear the hurt in her mother's voice, along with a little quiver. Even though she'd married into the Sherwood family, you'd never know it. Sherwood Enterprises was her lifeblood.

And now her mother had developed a sixth sense. How did she know that it had crossed her mind to leave Sherwood altogether?

"I...don't...know." She took a deep breath. "Mother, if I decide to leave Sherwood, I'll give you and father plenty of notice. I'll even help you find someone to take my place and will train the person for an easy transition. Please don't worry."

"This isn't like you, Marigold."

Mari sighed. "I know."

"I am most definitely worried about you, and not just in relation to the business. You're my daughter, and I don't want anything to happen to you in the mountains. But Hawk's Lake is a nice place. I enjoyed my time there."

This couldn't be her mother on the phone—the same person who came to Sherwood Lodge for a month in the summer under protest, and who couldn't wait to get back to Boston.

As they said their goodbyes, Mari felt better. At least her mother now knew, and her father soon would, that Mari was thinking of not accepting the job—and might not continue to work at the company at all. More important, her mother seemed to accept Mari's decision. Well, mostly.

Yet it was just too easy, and Mari was sure that this wasn't the end of the discussion.

She cleaned up the kitchen, stored the cookies in plastic bags and then filled the wheelbarrow with more of her pieces to be fired. Then she was going to go outside on her lawn chair, with her sketch pad and her pencils, to play with some designs for her pottery. Maybe draw some loons or trout.

Trout. That was one way to take her mind off her problems.

And that meant Brian. But did she want to reel him in, or throw him back?

The rising sun was burning off the fog, and Brian knew that it was going to be another unseasonably hot, sunny day. He didn't want to spend it all indoors.

He thought he'd pay a visit to Mari, since she hadn't answered her phone when he called to see how she was feeling.

He knew she was okay, so he didn't worry. This was a small town, after all, and word got around. She'd stopped at the bakery and the library yesterday.

Obviously, she was feeling better but didn't want to talk to him. Why?

He walked over to his heaped desk at the garage, and made neat piles—one for Jack to handle, another for Melanie, and even one for his father. By the time it took him to write a note with instructions for each stack, he could have done the job himself, but he might as well get them used to his absence.

Even if the Sherwood job didn't work out, he'd planned on applying to other companies that he'd been researching. On his short list was his old brokerage firm in New York where he'd worked after college. He kept in touch with a lot of the people there, particularly his old boss.

When he was gone, his family would have to learn how to take care of the business. He'd teach them—hell, he'd even hire someone for them.

But he'd miss all of them—foibles and all.

As he locked the door behind him, he made a mental note to gather his family together soon and tell them what he was planning.

He unlocked the latches and hit the button to put the top down on his convertible. Slipping in, he drove to his real-estate office. His desk there was even more piled with work, mail and letters.

He noticed the half-revised resumé he'd printed out was on his desk. He picked it up, looked at it and then laid it on top of a cover letter he'd prepared for Tom and Barbara Sherwood a few days ago.

Brian wondered why he didn't want to finish the damn thing. Maybe it was because Mari really hadn't given him a definite answer as to whether or not she was accepting the CEO job. He didn't want to step on her toes.

Mari. Every time he thought of her, he'd relive

the feel of her silky skin. The softness of her lips. How it felt to be inside her.

He awoke every morning thinking of her, went to bed every night wanting her beside him.

During the day, he could barely concentrate on the myriad of things he had to do. Instead he kept wondering what Mari was doing.

He just wanted to be with her all the time—talking, laughing and watching how her face glowed when she saw a family of ducks or talked about her pottery.

And now he'd remember the blush of pleasure on her face as they'd made love.

Picking up his incomplete resumé, he shook his head. He cared very much for Mari, and if she stayed in Hawk's Lake and he moved on, he just couldn't imagine leaving her.

He'd given up his dreams for his family before, but could he give up his dreams yet again—this time for love?

Chapter Eleven

Mari was on her way to the boathouse to fire some new pieces when she saw the flash of Brian's convertible out of the corner of her eye. A twinge of excitement rushed through her, followed by a twinge of suspicion.

She didn't know if she could stand him asking her about her job again. But if he did, she'd keep her cool and be on her toes.

He beeped his horn, and she nodded in his direction. While she was loading the kiln, Brian walked into the boathouse.

"Morning, Mari. Glad to see you're feeling better."

His black hair moved from the breeze off the lake, and he looked gorgeous, as usual.

He was casually dressed today—cargo shorts in his favorite color, khaki, along with hiking boots with short socks and a light blue shirt. Even when dressed down, he made her heart pound.

"Thanks." She decided to keep things light and breezy. "No work today? Is it a national holiday or something?"

He reached out to pull her into a kiss, but she offered him her cheek instead. He moved his head to capture her lips, but she stepped away.

Shifting his feet, Brian stuffed his hands into his pockets. She'd obviously made him uncomfortable. She regretted that, but she couldn't help herself.

"Something wrong?" he asked. "You're kind of…distant today."

"Nothing. I'm fine." She really felt fine—but also felt the need to be cautious.

"Okay. Whatever you say." He raised an eyebrow, obviously not believing her. "I think I'll go hiking up Old Baldy. I hate to be inside on such a nice day." He headed to his car.

She didn't want him to leave under these circumstances, but they needed time apart.

"Oh." He turned toward her. "I stopped in at three of my favorite gift shops in the area—the high-end ones. All three are very eager to sell your pottery." He paused. "I was going to ask you if you wanted to go hiking with me and celebrate with a picnic, but I guess you're not in the mood."

She watched as he got into his car and drove off, feeling even more miserable.

She should feel elated—his news announced her first sale of her own work as an artist. But she'd hurt him, and that was the last thing she wanted to do. She didn't know how to sort out her feelings in her own mind, so how on earth could she explain them to Brian?

Mari walked over to her lawn chair and stared at the lake, thinking. She could run Sherwood Enterprises, but she couldn't handle her personal life.

She did at least owe Brian a thank-you for finding outlets for her pottery. After all, he'd made it all possible. What would the harm be in driving up to Old Baldy and talking to him?

Mari hiked the entire trail to the top of the small mountain. Unless Brian strayed from the path, which he could have, he wasn't around.

Then she remembered that there was a path that

led to a waterfall that only the locals knew about. She hadn't been there in years. Could she find the path? She looked around, trying to remember. Finally, she saw it and backtracked, and eventually found Brian sitting on a boulder staring out at the waterfall.

"Brian?"

He spun around. "What on earth are you doing here? How did you find me?"

"I'm sorry. I didn't mean to startle you."

His voice still had an edge to it, but at least he was talking to her.

She walked toward him. "All the way up here, I was thinking about the time your dad took us all hiking. I had to have been about ten. I remember how we stood under the waterfall and let it pound us…." She laughed. "And we swung on ropes and fell into the water."

"I remember," he said quietly.

"Can I join you?" she asked.

"Suit yourself."

She took her backpack off, pulled out a plastic bag of her cookies and handed it to him. "A peace offering." She sat on a rock. "And I want to thank you for everything you did for my pottery business."

"You didn't have to come all the way out here to do that. Besides, that's what friends are for."

Mari was surprised to hear that he still considered her a friend. She could live with that, although in her heart of hearts, she wanted to believe that he didn't have another agenda.

"The shop owners must trust you," she said, wishing that she could trust him so blindly. "They didn't even know my work."

"It had nothing to do with me, Mari. Remember those two mugs you gave me? The ones with the ducks on it and the heron?"

"Sure."

"They loved the look and the detail on the pottery. The White Dove will take anything and everything. The owner, Mavis, wants an area exclusive. You'll like her." He smiled slightly. "Likewise with Adirondack Annie's in Raquette Lake and Gold Medal Gifts in Lake Placid. I tentatively negotiated for a ten-percent commission for each store, pending your approval. I asked around, and some gift-shop owners want fifteen percent."

"This is so exciting," she said. "I wish I had a bigger kiln."

"Don't worry. I made it clear that you didn't want to make this a big business—that you were an artist, and didn't mass-produce. Each piece is an original."

Mari couldn't believe the trouble and time he'd expended.

He munched on a cookie. "These are delicious. Is there anything that you can't do, Mari?"

I can't pick a man who loves me for who I am and not for what I can do for him.

She smiled in answer to his question.

"Brian, I need to tell you something." She took a deep breath. "I'm having a problem trusting you."

He began to speak, but she held up her hand. "Please, let me finish.

"I told you about the three guys who used me to get ahead at Sherwood."

"I remember."

"Well…I don't want you to be the fourth."

"Mari—"

"Are you romancing me because you want something?"

He looked at her as if she was speaking a foreign language. "Yes. I am."

Her heart sank. She'd told the truth, and obviously he was reciprocating.

"I want *you.* That's all, Mari. Just you."

Her heart soared. But could she believe him?

"I would never want to do anything to hurt

you. And as for trusting me—only you can decide to do that."

"Fair enough," she said. He made everything seem so simple.

Brian smiled. "Anything else bothering you?"

"I'm not going to return to Sherwood Enterprises at all. I want to move to Hawk's Lake." She looked pointedly at him. "But I'd appreciate it if you kept this between us until I have an opportunity to talk to my parents."

"Sure. I won't breathe a word to anyone. Pirate's promise."

She smiled at that, then looked over at the waterfall. There was silence between them, then Brian asked, "Are you sure, Mari? Really sure?"

"I'm sure. And I'm relieved. I feel…lighter and happier, now that I've decided, but I'm not looking forward to telling my parents and Grandma Rose. I just don't want them to be disappointed." She picked up a pebble and tossed it around in her hand. "I did clue in my mother a little when she phoned recently." She met his gaze. "She suspected that I wasn't happy lately, but for the most part they thought I came here to get over my latest failed engagement."

"I hope you'll be happy here, Mari." He took her

hand. "I have some news myself." He patted her hand. "I'm going to be moving on."

Ice settled in the pit of her stomach. "Moving on?"

"Time for me to return to my career path. And I have you to thank."

"*Me?* What on earth did I do?"

"You've reminded me of what I missed. You've had the job—the career—I've always wanted. And you've inspired me to go after it."

Mari felt like she couldn't breathe. She was staying, and Brian was leaving.

No. He couldn't.

"When?"

"Just as soon as something comes through. I still talk to my old boss, so I might just see if he's got any openings. And I have a short list of other places I'm going to apply to."

Excitement shimmered in his eyes. She should be happy for him, happy for herself. She'd finally made a decision, but inside she felt empty, hollow. Like a part of her was missing.

"Want to walk along the falls?" Brian held out his hand and she took it. A tingle shot up her arm at his touch, and she didn't want to let go. She didn't have much time with him.

Again, they were going to say goodbye.

They walked hand in hand down the worn path. Mari tried to enjoy the scenery and the calming sound of the water cascading into a small, secluded pool, but all she could think of was that she wouldn't have Brian to share it with much longer.

He squeezed her hand. "I happen to know a good real-estate agent. I'll bet he'd sell you Sherwood Lodge."

"Oh, Brian! Sold!"

It was a small consolation. She'd lose Brian, but she'd gain Sherwood Lodge. Her treasured cottage could never quite make up for the loss of the man who was about to walk out of her life for the second time.

When Brian realized he'd be losing Mari—again—he didn't feel as good about his decision as he'd thought he would.

"Let's sit here." He pointed to a nice grassy spot and they sat down. "One good thing about being my own boss is that I can do something like this on the spur of the moment."

"That's very true." She nodded. "So tell me why Hawk's Lake doesn't satisfy you professionally."

"It's so peaceful and serene here. I mean, there's nothing about Hawk's Lake that gets my heart racing. Nothing high stakes."

"No prematurely gray hair. No heart attack." She touched his wrist. "Sorry, I'll shut up. Please, go on."

"Look, you can't understand where I'm coming from. Maybe if you grew up in a small town where there's no big business, you'd understand why I've always wanted to work on Wall Street. I want to be a mover and shaker in the finance world. That's why I went to college. That's my thing, my dream."

"And Hawk's Lake doesn't need a financial whiz in residence?"

"Hardly." He shook his head. "Besides, it wouldn't be the same. It wouldn't have the excitement, the buzz, the intensity, even the competition with other people all racing for the same brass ring. And I've always wanted the challenge of climbing the corporate ladder, of getting to the top. Here, I'm just a one-man band. I miss all that craziness."

Mari took a deep breath. "I don't want to sound like I'm lecturing you—which of course I am—but being at the top of the ladder is not all wheeling and dealing. Have you ever told a couple hundred people that you had to lay them off in January? Now, that's a nice Christmas present."

"Mari, I know that it's not all fun and games, but being in the mix of things has always been my dream. It's *always* been what I wanted to do."

"But, Brian, you *are* in the mix of things. You have a hand in improving the lives of everyone in Hawk's Lake. Do you think any hotshot CEO has that kind of power? That kind of influence? You impact everyone's life on such a personal basis, day to day. Why can't you see that?"

Damn. Could Mari be right?

No way. She meant well, but she was wrong. He just helped out the village whenever he could, but he'd never meant to stay here.

Hawk's Lake was never his dream.

Mari played with a blade of grass. "I'll miss you, you know."

Maybe. But he'd miss her more.

What was he doing? They'd just found each other again after all these years. How could he walk away from her again?

He loved being with her. He loved everything about her.

But he owed it to himself to take a real shot at achieving his dream.

He could never ask her to join him—her heart wasn't in the corporate world anymore. She wanted peaceful and serene—she'd already made that clear. He wanted action.

This was his chance. Maybe his last chance.

Other couples had long-distance relationships— so could they. With e-mail, cell phones, cameras on computers and other technology, they could easily keep in touch.

"If I land in New York or Boston, I won't be that far away."

"Yes, you will," Mari said, her eyes turned toward the waterfall. "It's twelve years from here."

"But we're together now, Mari, and we should make the most of our time together," Brian said.

He leaned over to kiss her, and for a moment he could see a little sadness in her face, but it faded. She slipped her arms around his neck. Then her fingers brushed back his hair and their lips met.

He pulled her down to the new spring grass blanketed with mist. He studied her face, cupped her cheek with his hand. She was his Marigold. His beautiful flower.

He loved her. He probably always had loved her, and he'd picked a damn fine time to realize that— now, when he was about to leave.

But they were at opposite ends of the spectrum. Right now, he and Mari wanted different things.

He pushed all that from his mind. He couldn't wait to feel her soft, warm skin against his. Moving her to his side, he pulled up her T-shirt and tossed it. He pushed up her bra and kissed her perfect breasts, playing with her nipples with his tongue.

He quickly got rid of the rest of his clothes, found a condom in his wallet and said a quick prayer that no one else would be visiting the falls this early in the season.

With the sound of the water roaring in his ears and the heat of the sun on his back, he made slow, seductive love to Mari. And when he entered her and finally let himself go, he knew this was the woman he'd been waiting for his whole life.

And the woman he was going to leave behind—again.

Chapter Twelve

They said their goodbyes at the parking lot by the trailhead.

"Do you want to meet me for dinner later?" he asked. "I have to make a quick stop at the office to pick up some paperwork, and then drive to Thendara—the buyers want to do a final inspection on a property—but it shouldn't take me more than three hours, if everything goes as planned," he said. "I'll call you when I'm done."

"I'd love to. I'll meet you at Aunt Betty's Pancake House."

Mari drove back to Sherwood Lodge, thinking about her wonderful afternoon with Brian. It had been so romantic—a picnic by the waterfalls, a nice talk with him, so that they straightened things out between them, and then they made love. And as the sun made a rainbow over the falls, Mari knew without a doubt that she loved Brian.

This would be the place that she'd love to raise her children. But that wasn't going to happen.

A heaviness descended on her heart. Could she live in Hawk's Lake without Brian?

It wouldn't be the same.

She'd spent a lot of energy trying to keep her distance from him on this vacation. She wished she could have that time back, since she didn't have much time left.

Mari heard the phone ringing inside the cottage just as she got out of the van. It couldn't be Brian. He wasn't even near Thendara yet, unless he'd stopped at a pay phone to call her.

The faster she struggled to open the door, the more she fumbled. Finally, she was inside and running to the kitchen.

"Hello."

"Marigold, it's your mother. I have something to tell you." She took a breath. "Your father had a heart attack. He just had a quadruple bypass, and he made it through just fine. I would have called you sooner, but everything happened so fast."

Her mother's news didn't quite register. Tom Sherwood had such vigor and energy that no one could keep up with him.

"Will he be okay?" Mari asked, her voice cracking.

"The doctor is optimistic. Since your father…"

Her mother was crying. Her mother never cried. Mari could tell that she was trying to control herself.

"Since your father is in otherwise good shape."

"I'm coming home, Mom. It'll only take me a few hours. Don't worry about Dad. He'll be fine." Mari didn't know what else to say. "Where is he now?"

"In recovery. Then he'll be moved to cardiac care. I know he'll be okay." Her mother's voice quivered. "But he looked so sick…so helpless. And I'm not used to seeing him that way."

"Is Grandma with you?"

"Yes."

"Where are you?"

"At Beacon of Light Hospital on Fourth Street, in the waiting room of the cardiac care unit." She could hear her mother talking to someone, but couldn't make out the words. "I have to go now, Mari. The doctor is here."

"Okay, I'll call you as soon as I'm able to get reception on my cell phone."

"Drive carefully, Mari."

She heard a click, and Mari stood in the kitchen, surrounded by darkness and silence, deciding that she wouldn't panic, couldn't panic.

She ran upstairs, slipped into jeans and pulled a sweatshirt on. Grabbing a jacket and her purse, she turned off all the lights and locked the cottage behind her. On the side porch, she pulled the plug on her pottery wheel and locked the door of the porch. Running to the boathouse, she pulled the plug on her kiln. Then she ran to the van.

Dialing Brian on her cell phone, she hoped against hope that she could get him. She couldn't.

Driving as fast as she dared, she steered the van down the dark, curvy road that ran behind the cottages and onto Route 28. She had to drive by his real-estate office. Maybe she could catch him there. More likely, she'd just leave him a note that she was going home and that she'd return as soon as her father was stable.

It was difficult to concentrate on the narrow, twisting mountain road, but she didn't want to run off the road like the busload of senior tourists.

The lights weren't on in the office, but the lights

were on upstairs. She rang the doorbell. After a few seconds, she heard a window open above her.

"Hello? Who's there?" It was Mrs. Newley.

Mari ran down the porch steps and looked up. "It's Marigold Sherwood, Mrs. Newley. I'm so sorry to bother you, but it's a bit of an emergency. I'd like to leave a note for Brian. Can I come in?"

"Sure. I'll be right down."

The lights went on and the door opened.

"Is everything all right, dear?"

"No, I have to go home to Boston. My father had a heart attack and just had emergency surgery. I'd like to leave Brian some phone numbers where I can be reached."

"I'm sure your father will be fine. Try not to worry too much." She waved Mari on. "Go leave a note on his desk. The light switch is on the wall. Can I make you something for the road, Mari? It's a long ride."

"I'm fine. But would you mind trying to find Brian and telling him where I've gone? I was supposed to meet him for dinner at Aunt Betty's, but I have to leave, and—"

"I'll let him know, Mari."

Mari turned the light on in Brian's office and couldn't believe the mess. Folders and papers were stacked everywhere and the stacks tipped at precarious angles. Some had already hit the floor. Others were ready to slide like an avalanche onto a new location. Pink message forms were scattered like confetti.

His office was a dump.

In spite of worrying about her father, she felt a tiny tinge of satisfaction. Obviously, Brian wasn't as in control as he made himself out to be.

She flipped the pages on a yellow tablet to a clean page, grabbed a pen from the cup on his desk and wrote a quick note.

She listed the numbers for her apartment, her office and her cell. Taking the keys out of her pocket, she set them on her note. Then a piece of paper caught her eye—a letter addressed to her parents. With shaking hands, she picked it up and skimmed it.

I'd like to apply for the position of CEO…resumé is attached…happy to appear for a personal interview…thank you for…

His resumé was on his desk, too, and it looked like everything was ready to be mailed.

There it was in black and white. He was applying for her job. He probably couldn't wait to get back to his office and write that letter. No wonder he

kept asking her if she was going to take the job—
he wanted to get a jump on the competition.

Her heart constricted painfully. After all his talk
that he only wanted *her*...

He'd lied.

And here she'd been, hoping that he'd give up his
dream and that they could build something great
together. But it didn't look like Brian was ready—
or that he'd ever be ready.

He was just another corporate climber.

Tears stung her eyes as she stuffed both docu-
ments into her purse. With one look back at his
desk, she left.

Is this closing ever going to end?

Brian secretively looked at his watch as the three
sisters who were buying the old ski shop checked the
bank's figures on a calculator the size of a credit card.

They planned on turning the building into a
Christmas store and living above it in a small apartment. They were very nice ladies, probably in their
mid fifties or early sixties, and would be a nice asset
to Hawk's Lake. Two were widows, and one said
she was "still looking for a very rich man."

Finally, everything was signed, checks were
written and keys were distributed.

When they started measuring for curtains, Brian said his goodbyes and stopped at a gas station to call Mari. No answer.

Maybe she was in the boathouse doing something with her pottery.

He headed north on Route 28. Along the way, he stopped at a pay phone at the driveway leading to the Hemlock Acres Campground and called again. Still no answer.

Back on the road, he didn't stop again until he was at Aunt Betty's. He used the pay phone inside the restaurant. No answer again.

He sat at a table, tapping his fingers, getting more worried with each passing minute of their ridiculous moose clock. Mari knew he was going to call. Where could she be?

What should he do? He waited for what seemed like an eternity and called again. Nothing.

He decided to drive out to Sherwood Lodge to check on her.

Dammit. He was going to work day and night to make sure that a cell tower was installed in these mountains and that it would be able to transmit to every nook and cranny of Hawk's Lake. Then he'd work on service to the entire Adirondack Preserve.

Suddenly, he almost couldn't breathe, couldn't

swallow. Mari was right—Hawk's Lake *was* like his own personal corporation.

He could do whatever he wanted to improve the place in which he grew up. He could make the cell tower happen, make anything happen, just like he always had.

Just this afternoon she'd pointed out that he'd already achieved his dream. It hadn't sunk in then. It took something like no cell phone service to wake him up and make him realize that she was absolutely right.

Or was it because he couldn't connect with the person who had come to mean the most to him? The woman he loved. The woman he'd *always* loved.

And he was worried sick about her. Why didn't she answer?

Sherwood Lodge was in sight now. It was completely dark and Mari's van was gone.

Where could she be?

With his heart pounding, he drove right onto the lawn and up to the side door of Sherwood Lodge. He found the extra key that he had hidden and opened the door. She wasn't on the porch.

He opened the inside door. "Mari? Mari!"

Turning on lights, he raced from one room to another, then took off across the lawn to check the boathouse. But that, too, was empty, and he noticed that her kiln was unplugged.

Puzzled, Brian slumped into a chair. Just as he was about to call the police, the phone rang in the kitchen.

He answered on the second ring. "Hello?"

"Brian, thank goodness I found you. I've been trying everywhere and thought you might be there."

"Mrs. Newley? What's wrong? Do you know—"

"Mari's father had a heart attack. He's had emergency bypass surgery. That's all I know. Mari's gone back home, but she left you a note on your desk."

Relief washed over him. Surrounded by Mari's pottery, he thought about how much he'd looked forward to being with her this evening. He said a quick prayer that she'd be okay driving alone throughout the night.

She had to be exhausted. He wished he could call her—to hear her voice and to reassure her that her father would be fine. At least, he hoped that would be the case.

And he hoped that he and Mari would be able to work things through—together.

Chapter Thirteen

The gas gauge was near empty, so Mari finally pulled into a service station to fill up her tank.

She called her mother's cell phone, then realized that if she was at the hospital her phone was probably turned off due to regulations. She left a message.

She wanted to call Brian, too, but then remembered the papers in her purse. As much as it hurt her to admit, Brian didn't love her. He'd wanted her job—not her—all along.

It was a bad time to tell her parents that she was

definitely going to resign from Sherwood Enterprises and move to Hawk's Lake. She needed to postpone her news until her father's crisis was over.

The gas pump clicked off and Mari capped the tank and paid the cashier. After buying a bottle of water from the soda machine, she was back on the road. She hoped to arrive in Boston at about three o'clock in the morning.

Twenty miles from the Massachusetts border, doubts began to sneak in. Maybe Brian hadn't tried to use her to get a jump on her job. Maybe she was just blowing things out of proportion.

He'd admitted he was applying at several places, but still, he'd never mentioned Sherwood as one of them. Why not?

Mari reached down and found a radio station. The blast of hard rock filled the car. She cranked up the volume.

Damn. She needed to stop questioning her instincts. She knew what Brian was up to. She'd seen the evidence with her own eyes. Now it was in her purse. And he'd even promised not to tip off her parents until she had a chance to talk with them. Obviously Brian was no better than any of the other men who had used her to carve out a career for themselves.

Her fingers tightened on the steering wheel until her hands ached.

Reaching down, she scanned the channels until she found a classical station. The sweet, calming notes slid out of the speakers and slowed the hard, angry beat of her heart.

Her hands relaxed and her shoulders loosened. A deep breath slipped from between her lips.

What was she doing to herself? Every thought of Brian was tying her into a thousand knots.

Turquoise eyes that were full of concern flashed into her consciousness. How could she dismiss the care she'd seen in his eyes—on his face—when they'd made love?

Who was she to say that all those things meant nothing—that they were a lie? She couldn't—wouldn't—believe that.

But what more evidence did she need?

Anger flared again. She changed the station back to rock as she pushed Brian out of her thoughts and out of her life. He didn't warrant one more second of her time. She needed to forget him—for good.

Brian woke up when he heard voices in the main part of Hawkins's Garage. He remembered putting his head down on the desk, just to rest his eyes, but he must have dozed off.

He checked the clock—seven in the morning.

He was hoping that Mari would call. But he hadn't heard from her. She must have been busy with her father.

Brian got up, stretched and headed to the men's room. When he returned, Melanie and Jack were there. Melanie was sitting at his desk. Jack was on the other side, leaning back with his feet up. The smell of coffee permeated the air, and he helped himself from the pot.

Melanie grinned at him. "Look what the cat wouldn't even drag in. The cat probably didn't recognize you without your suit on."

"I knew there was a reason why I didn't recognize you." Jack snapped his fingers. "You must be cleaning the village sewers or something today." Then he rubbed his chin. "Naw. You'd wear your suit for that."

Brian collapsed in a chair next to Jack. "Okay, have your fun."

Melanie took a sip of coffee. "We wouldn't dream of picking on you. You might leave more work for us to do." She looked over Jack's shoulder. "How's Mari?"

"I don't really know. She had to go home. Her father had a heart attack."

Melanie closed her eyes. "Oh, no. Is he okay?"

"I don't know for sure. He had emergency surgery."

"Give her our best," Melanie said.

"I will," Brian said. "When I see her." He was quiet for a minute. "You know, I miss her. Mari hasn't been gone twenty-four hours yet, and I miss her."

"So why aren't you in Boston at her side?" Melanie asked.

"It's complicated."

"So make it simple," Jack said.

"She's going to quit her family's company and live in Hawk's Lake," Brian said.

Jack raised an eyebrow. "So far, I don't see a problem."

"I've always wanted to leave Hawk's Lake—it's always been my dream. I was going to ask Mari to put in a good word for me with her parents—maybe put me in the running for the CEO job. If that didn't work out, I thought I'd try to go back to my old job at the brokerage." He rubbed his forehead. "But now I don't know." He looked at Jack, then at Melanie. Neither of them was reacting. "Mari complicated everything."

"That you weren't happy here is news to me, Brian," Melanie said. "Why didn't you go back?"

"News to me, too," Jack echoed. "Why didn't you ever tell us?"

Brian couldn't believe they were so clueless. "Oh, come on. I couldn't leave. There was one thing after another to deal with, and everything always fell to me. Melanie, you had problems. We did two expansions on the garage. The books were a mess. Jack, you were never here to take care of anything. I *had* to stay."

Melanie and Jack looked at each other. They were obviously puzzled.

What didn't they get?

Melanie was the first to speak. "Brian, you could have left anytime you wanted. No one kept you here. We would have gotten things done, somehow, without you."

Jack nodded. "If you'd ever told me how you felt, I would have stopped racing and would have been here."

Melanie's shoulders slumped. "I never knew you were unhappy, Brian. I was caught up in my own problems, for sure—with Mike's death and taking care of Kyle—but you never seemed like you were in a hurry to go back to New York City. Matter of fact, you seemed to make excuses *not* to go back."

Brian's head was reeling. Were they right? Had he made excuses not to go back?

He stared at his coffee as if the answer was waiting for him at the bottom of the cup, the answer that would straighten out his whole life.

"You love her, don't you?" Melanie asked.

Brian was shocked. "H-How did you know?"

"You've *always* loved her, Bri." Melanie looked astonished that he'd even ask such an inane question. "Have you told her how you feel?"

"Uh...no. Not yet."

"Do you think that would be something she'd want to know?" Melanie asked, eyes wide. "I certainly would!"

"Get going," Jack said. "Don't think for once, Brian. Don't tally up the columns. Just hop in your car, buckle up and go. And don't speed."

Melanie stood. "And don't worry about a thing here. That's what family is for."

They walked him to his car, kissed and hugged him and wished him well.

He turned onto the highway and headed to Boston.

Chapter Fourteen

Mari dozed in an orange vinyl chair in the cramped cardiac care waiting room.

Only one person was able to see her father—for five minutes out of the hour. Her grandmother had just returned. Then it would be her turn.

She'd never seen her mother look so tired and helpless. When Mari had walked into the waiting room, her mother had clung to her like a lifeline.

"I'm so glad you're here, Mari," she'd said.

"How's Daddy?"

"He's sleeping. I just sat there and held his hand.

The doctor said that everything was going to be fine. The bypass went well." Her mother started to sob. This was the first time that Mari ever remembered seeing her mother cry, and she seemed so old, so frail. Her mother reached for her again, and Mari rubbed her back, trying to remember the last time they had hugged.

Grandma Rose held a crumpled white handkerchief in her hand, and she was dabbing at her eyes. The three women huddled together on the couch, presenting a united front, as they always had.

"I thought I lost him," her mother said, composing herself. "Thank goodness he's going to be okay."

"He'll be fine, Barbara. He's a Sherwood," Grandma proclaimed as fact. "How was your trip to the lake, Mari? Did you have a good time?"

"I did. I enjoyed it very much, and our cottage looked…the same. It's still magnificent."

"That place always held a special place in your heart," her mother said, taking her hand and squeezing it.

Maybe it wouldn't be so special, now that Brian Hawkins was leaving. Mari tightened her hands together and squeezed the thought into nonexistence.

"I've missed you," her mother said.

Her mother had never said that—then again, Mari had never taken a vacation. "Thanks, Mom. I've missed you, too."

Grandma exchanged her old handkerchief for a new one and looked at Mari through red-rimmed eyes. "Your mother tells me that you've become re-acquainted with Brian Hawkins. You two were inseparable as far back as I can remember."

Mari wanted to scream, but instead she simply nodded. "It was a little too cold yet to swim, but we did go boating and hiking, and I made pottery—just like you showed me, Grandma. Remember?" Mari tried to steer the conversation away from Brian. She was still too raw from his betrayal.

"I do. Just like my mother showed me, and her mother showed her." Rose took Mari's other hand. "There's a lot of your great-grandmother in you, Mari. Have I ever told you that?"

Her grandmother's words released a wave of guilt that washed over her. How could she tell them that she didn't want to run the company anymore? With her father in intensive care and her mother an emotional wreck, the family needed her as the head of Sherwood more than ever.

Now was not the time to turn her back on them because she thought she wanted to drop out of the fast lane and disappear into a small Adirondack town to make her pottery.

It seemed as if the weight of the whole company had settled squarely on her shoulders.

She started ticking things off in her mind, then decided she needed a paper and pen to write everything down. Opening her purse, she pulled out two sheets of folded white paper. Perfect. Then she fumbled in her purse and pulled out a pen.

"Is that anything important you're about to write on, Mari?" her mother asked, pointing to the typing on the back.

Distracted, Mari zipped her purse before everything fell out. "What did you say, Mother?"

"What are you writing on?"

Mari looked at the paper. As soon as she saw the printed heading at the top of the sheet, she wanted to groan. No matter how hard she tried, she couldn't seem to get away from Brian Hawkins. She'd forgotten that she'd stuffed his resumé and cover letter into her purse.

She sighed and refolded the paper. "It's Brian Hawkins's resumé. He wants to work for Sherwood. I think he'd be great."

Brian wanted the job so damn much, he'd give it

his all. He ran Hawk's Lake like a CEO, so what was the difference? Let him have it.

"But we can talk about Brian and Sherwood at another time." Mari could barely finish her sentence when the tears came. She tried to wipe them away before they were noticed, but her mother didn't miss a thing.

"What's the matter?"

"Oh, everything. I'm worried about Daddy. And then there's B-Brian and the company." She desperately wiped at the corners of her eyes, feeling like a total fool. Why did she let him get to her like this? When would she ever learn? "I'm sorry. I guess I'm more tired than I thought. I'll be okay."

Her grandmother handed her a clean handkerchief. "Your father will be fine. And he has wonderful doctors. What about Brian? Tell us what's bothering you."

"It's not the right time, Gram."

Her mother brushed Mari's hair back. "There's nothing else to do here but talk—and worry—and I'm exhausted from worrying. So let's talk. Tell us."

Mari took a deep breath. "I've decided not to return to Sherwood. I'm sorry to let you both down and to let Daddy down. I'll stay and run the company until he's okay and back at work, but then I want out. This just isn't the life I want for myself. I'm so sorry to let you down."

Her mother and grandmother were silent for a moment.

"I suspected this for a long time, Mari," her mother said quietly. "We all did. You didn't have your heart in the company anymore. And when you finally decided to take a vacation for two months, at first we thought it was due to your breakup with Jason. But you've always bounced back from your breakups."

If she only knew...

"But, Mari, if you were tired of Sherwood or wanted out, why didn't you say something?" asked Grandma Rose.

"I went to Hawk's Lake to think—about a lot of things. Mostly I realized that it's hard to walk away from my heritage—my family. After all, Sherwood was passed down to me from all the Sherwood women and Daddy. And now he's ill. And I'm it. I'm the only one left."

She stopped for a breath and noticed her mother and grandmother staring at her, mouths open.

Her grandmother recovered first. "Sweetie, whether or not you run the company, you'll always be a part of it. If Violet and Iris were here, they would never want you to be unhappy, and neither do I. Sherwood Enterprises will always be your heritage." She tucked a strand of hair behind Mari's ear and smiled. "And you will always be our best-selling china pattern, Marigold."

Mari laughed. "I know. I outsell you, Grandma, two to one."

"Oh, you two!" Her mother laughed, then patted Mari's hand. "Sweetie, please don't let your father's illness influence your decision. You're my daughter first and I want you to be happy. So does your father."

Grandma Rose nodded. "Absolutely."

Her mother slid her hand into Mari's. "In light of your father's heart attack, I have come to several conclusions myself. A wake-up call like a serious illness makes you think of all the things you've done wrong. One of those things I'd like to change would be to spend more time with you, if it's not too late. We neglected you when you were growing up because of the company, and that's going to stop now."

Mari was stunned. "Oh, Mom! I'd love to spend more time with you and Daddy. And it's not too late. I understand." And she did.

A look of such love and tenderness filled her mother's face that, for a moment, Mari felt a flash of those sweet summer nights when her mother would tuck her into bed. Safe and content in her upstairs room at Sherwood Lodge, she'd listen to the soft hum of her parents' voices as they talked on the porch below.

Her mother reached up and gently touched her cheek. "I have a feeling that somehow I raised a daughter who won't make the same foolish mistakes with her children as I did."

Tears stung Mari's eyes when she realized that she'd probably never have her own family.

They were interrupted when a nurse appeared at the waiting room door. "Mr. Sherwood is awake now. He's asking for Barbara."

Her mother turned to her.

"It's your turn, Mari."

"Go ahead, Mom. He's asking for you. Just tell him I'm here."

She gave Mari a kiss on the cheek. "I will."

Brian tried to navigate the streets of downtown Boston, but he was half-stuck at the intersection, as horns blared and pedestrians swarmed all around his convertible trying to get around him. With more horns blaring, he tried to study his global mapping device.

A cabdriver pulled up alongside him. "What are you looking for, pal?"

He looked at the scribbled paper where he'd written down the address of the hospital. Mari's assistant, Julie, had given him directions, too, but about now, nothing made any sense.

"Fourth and Hope," Brian said. "Beacon of Light Hospital."

"This is your lucky day. Follow me. I'm headed there now."

"Thanks."

Brian squeezed in behind the taxi. More horns blared.

"Give me a break," he yelled.

He looked around, keeping a close watch on the taxi's bumper. High-rise buildings as far as he could see stood like sentinels, one after the other, blocking out the sun. You could get claustrophobic in this place, he thought.

The noise and the smell of diesel from the buses were getting to him. He should have put up the top on his convertible. Too late. He didn't dare do it now, in this mess.

Strange. Things like high-rises and fumes had never bothered him before.

The same cars passed him, no doubt circling for a parking space.

He saw two mothers pushing strollers, trying to

cross the street. Holding his breath, he hoped no one would hit them.

He'd forgotten about *this* part of city life.

He checked his watch. It was two o'clock. The lunch-hour rush was probably over. He was starving, but he couldn't just pull over and run in somewhere. There was absolutely nowhere to park.

The taxi driver beeped his horn and pointed to a parking garage. Brian waved and turned into the lane heading to the garage. Amazed at the high prices, he hit the button for a card and circled up the ramp, looking for a space. Finally, he squeezed into a space on the top floor.

Grabbing his backpack, he followed the signs to the hospital and found himself in a packed elevator and a crowded lobby. People jostled him from every direction. At the tiny gift shop, he bought a couple of bouquets of flowers, then waited in line at the reception desk to find out where Thomas Sherwood's room was located.

After stops on every floor, he finally squeezed himself out of the elevator onto the eighth floor.

On his right, he saw Mari slowly pacing inside the glass-windowed waiting room of the cardiac care unit.

Brian watched her for a moment. Judging by the

droop of her shoulders and the way her brows furrowed, she was exhausted and worried.

He'd love to whisk her away to a hotel and make sure she got something to eat and some sleep, but he knew that Mari would never leave the hospital until she was sure that everything was okay.

Just then, she saw him. Her jaw dropped and her expression grew…blank.

Not quite the reaction he'd hoped for.

Mari couldn't believe her eyes as she ran out of the room. "Brian! What are you doing here?" she asked, her voice stiff.

Even as she reminded herself to keep her distance, her body warred with her mind. She wanted to take comfort in his warm embrace. She wanted to turn back time to before she'd learned that he was just like all the other men she'd known. Before he'd hurt her.

"I was worried about you, Mari."

"You shouldn't have come all this way just to check on me. You could have called." She tried to keep her tone blank—impersonal. Now was not the time to discuss their relationship—such as it was.

"But I wanted to be with you," Brian said, "to see what I could do to help. I thought you might need me."

His gaze measured her, and she could see the confusion—and hurt—in the depths of his blue eyes.

"How's your dad?"

"He's okay. The surgery went well. I haven't seen him yet. My mother's visiting him now."

"You look tired, Mari."

"And so do you, Brian. You look like you slept in those clothes." She raised an eyebrow.

"I did. I guess I had a certain lady on my mind."

She longed to take his hand, wanting to feel his warmth and strength. But instead she clenched her hands into fists behind her back. Now was the time to stay in control—the time to protect her heart from any further pain that came from loving a man who didn't want the same things as she did. A man who'd used her.

Still, he had come after her. That meant something, though she wasn't sure what, exactly. She supposed a little kindness was in order and nodded in the direction of the waiting room. "Why don't you join us. I'm sure my grandmother would like to see you again. My mother will be back soon."

Even to her own ears, her voice sounded formal, almost distant, as if he was someone from the company who had stopped by to pay his respects, instead of the man who, a short time ago, she'd made love with.

She introduced him to Grandma Rose, who gave him a big hug. "Of course I remember Brian."

Her mother walked in and there were more greetings. She shook his hand. "Thank you for spending time with Mari at the lake."

"It was my pleasure," he said, turning to give Mari a slight wink. Her cheeks heated at his innuendo.

They all made small talk until Brian said, "Mari, could I talk to you in private for a moment?"

Mari shrugged. "Sure. There's a little office on the other side of the hall. It's for clergy, but I think we can use it."

They walked over to the room. Mari took a seat, but he stood.

"What's wrong?" she asked, looking up.

Brian gazed at her intently. "Nothing. I just wanted to tell you that I don't want to leave Hawk's Lake. If you're going to live there, that's where I want to be."

Her eyebrows furrowed. "I don't understand."

"You were right about everything. I can do whatever I want in Hawk's Lake. And I could have gone back to Wall Street whenever I wanted, but I was making excuses to stay. I don't want to work at Sherwood or anywhere else, for that matter.

That's probably why I didn't mail out my resumés anywhere. I just couldn't bring myself to do it."

"You didn't plan on sending them?" she asked, just to make sure she understood him.

"At first I did, but then...*no.* Then I considered applying for your job. I was just waiting for you to decide before I acted. But I couldn't bring myself to go for that, either."

She pulled out his letter from her purse and held it up. "You weren't going to mail this?"

"No." He rubbed his head. "I didn't know you found that. You probably thought I was going to mail it before you had a chance to talk to your parents."

She met his gaze. "Of course."

"Check the date on that letter."

Mari did so. It was dated the day after she'd arrived in Hawk's Lake.

"Mari, please believe me. After we got to know each other again, I couldn't bring myself to go for your job, or any job for that matter. Not if it meant hurting you." He sighed. "You were right—about everything. I was living my dream in Hawk's Lake, but never knew."

Mari heard sincerity in Brian's voice—and realized she'd been wrong about him. Totally wrong.

"So, when are you going to trust me, Mari?"

"Now," she said firmly. "Right now."

"Good." Brian took her hand. "And you were right about something else, too—Hawk's Lake is the perfect place to raise children."

She felt hope swelling in her heart. Hope that the two of them could get another chance to start over.

"Are you telling me that you've changed your mind about Hawk's Lake, too, Brian?"

"You made me see everything clearly. I've already achieved my dream—I just didn't know it." He took a deep breath. "But there's still one person that I need to make it complete."

He handed her the flowers that she'd thought he'd brought for her father and knelt before her.

Her heart was pounding so loudly in her chest, she was sure that a nurse would come by and tell her to be quiet.

"This isn't exactly the most romantic place to ask you something important, but I can't wait another minute."

He slipped a cigar box out of his backpack.

It was the treasure chest that she'd made him when she was nine! It had lost some of its glitter and a few pennies had come off the sides, but to her it looked better than ever. She couldn't believe he had kept it all these years.

"Marigold Sherwood, I love you. Will you marry me and make me the happiest man in Hawk's Lake?"

He opened the cigar box and took out a ring—a tiny glass "diamond" ring with an adjustable metal band. He'd gotten it out of a gumball machine at Clancy's store when he was fourteen, and had given it to her.

"I thought I lost this in the lake."

"You did. I found it and forgot to give it back to you," Brian said.

As they had a thousand times over the years, her eyes immediately went to her ring finger. "That's the ring I've been looking for—waiting for—forever."

"I'll exchange it for a real one," he said. "Just say you love me and will marry me and live with me in Sherwood Lodge."

Hot, happy tears trailed a path down her cheeks. "Oh, Brian! Yes! Yes, I'll marry you!"

He slipped the ring onto her finger. There it was—the most spectacular ring she'd ever had. The one that had meant the most to her, and always would.

Brian raised his hand as if he was taking an oath, his eyes twinkling in merriment. "Pirate's promise that you'll marry me, and we'll live happily ever after in Hawk's Lake?"

She raised her hand and stifled a laugh. "Pirate's promise."

She pulled him to his feet, and they hugged each other. And when they kissed, they both knew they'd found their way home.

Epilogue

Two years later

It was a beautiful day for a family picnic, Brian thought, turning the sweet corn on the grill.

Melanie's daughter, Angie, was making sand pies on the beach with her father in front of Sherwood-Hawkins Lodge. Ed Hawkins was talking to Barb and Tom Sherwood and Grandma Rose as they all sipped lemonade and sat in white Adirondack chairs by the lake.

Jack and his latest girlfriend were out on the speedboat, pulling Kyle on a tube behind it.

Mari and Melanie were bringing salads out of the Lodge and setting them on the picnic table.

Brian could smell the scent of fresh lumber on the breeze, and he looked at the skeleton of the large addition he was constructing on the right side of their cottage. There would be an office for him, as well as a studio and office for Mari. Together they would run the Sherwood Foundation, a philanthropic and charitable organization, funded by the sale of Sherwood Enterprises to family friends. When she wasn't working for the fund, Mari was busy crafting her beautiful pottery, which often sold out at area gift shops.

Barbara and Tom had decided to do some traveling. No doubt, they would spend a lot of time in Hawk's Lake, just as soon as he and Mari made their big announcement at the bonfire tonight.

Grandma Rose would certainly spend a lot of time in Hawk's Lake, too, whenever she wasn't at her condo in Florida.

They were all more than welcome at the cottage. Mari and he certainly could use their help in about seven and a half months.

Mari must have sensed he was thinking about her

because her gaze met Brian's. She pointed to her stomach, where she carried their twin daughters.

Brian held up two fingers, and they both grinned.

Surrounded by everyone he loved, Brian knew that his life was perfect. After all, Mari had always been his perfect match.

* * * * *

Celebrate 60 years of pure reading
pleasure with Harlequin®!

Harlequin Presents® is proud to introduce its
gripping new miniseries,
THE ROYAL HOUSE OF KAREDES.
An exquisite coronation diamond,
split as a symbol of a warring
royal family's feud, is missing!
But whoever reunites the diamond halves
will rule all....

Welcome to eight brand-new titles that unfold to
reveal the stories of kings and queens, princes
and princesses torn apart by pride and power, but
finally reunited by love.

Step into the world of Karedes with
BILLIONAIRE PRINCE, PREGNANT
MISTRESS.
Available July 2009 from Harlequin Presents®.

ALEXANDROS KAREDES, SNOW DUSTING the shoulders of his leather jacket and glittering like jewels in his dark hair, stood at the door. Maria felt the blood drain from her head.

"Good evening, Ms. Santos."

His voice was as she remembered it. Deep. Husky. Perfect English, but with the faintest hint of a Greek accent. And cold, as cold as it had been that awful morning she would never forget, when he'd accused her of horrible things, called her terrible names....

"Aren't you going to ask me in?"

She fought for composure. Last time they'd faced each other, they'd been on his turf. Now they were on hers. She was in command here, and that meant everything.

"There's a sign on the door downstairs," she said, her tone every bit as frigid as his. "It says, 'No soliciting or vagrants.'"

His lips drew back in a wolfish grin. "Very amusing."

"What do you want, Prince Alexandros?"

A tight smile eased across his mouth and it killed her that even now, knowing he was a vicious, arrogant man, she couldn't help but notice what a handsome mouth it was. Chiseled. Generous. Beautiful, like the rest of him, which made him living proof that beauty could, indeed, be only skin-deep.

"Such formality, Maria. You were hardly so proper the last time we were together."

She knew his choice of words was deliberate. She felt her face heat; she couldn't help that but she damned well didn't have to let him lure her into a verbal sparring match.

"I'll ask you once more, your highness. What do you want?"

"Ask me in and I'll tell you."

"I have no intention of asking you in. Tell me

why you're here or don't. It's your choice, just as it will be my choice to shut the door in your face."

He laughed. It infuriated her but she could hardly blame him. He was tall—six-two, six-three—and though he stood with one shoulder leaning against the door frame, hands tucked casually into the pockets of the jacket, his pose was deceptive. He was strong, with the leanly muscled body of a well-trained athlete.

She remembered his body with painful clarity. The feel of him under her hands. The power of him moving over her. The taste of him on her tongue.

Suddenly, he straightened, his laughter gone. "I have not come this distance to stand in your doorway," he said coldly, "and I am not going to leave until I am ready to do so. I suggest you stand aside and stop behaving like a petulant child."

A petulant child? Was that what he thought? This man who had spent hours making love to her and had then accused her of—of trading her body for profit?

Except it had not been love, it had been sex. And the sooner she got rid of him, the better.

She let go of the doorknob and stepped aside. "You have five minutes."

He strolled past her, bringing cold air and the scent of the night with him. She swung toward him, arms folded. He reached past her, pushed the door closed, then folded his arms, too. She wanted to open the door again but she'd be damned if she was going to get into a who's-in-charge-here argument with him. She was in charge, and he would surely see a tussle over the ground rules as a sign of weakness.

Instead, she looked past him at the big clock above her worktable.

"Ten seconds gone," she said briskly. "You're wasting time, your highness."

"What I have to say will take longer than five minutes."

"Then you'll just have to learn to economize. More than five minutes, I'll call the police."

Instantly, his hand was wrapped around her wrist. He tugged her toward him, his dark chocolate eyes almost black with anger.

"You do that and I'll tell every tabloid shark I can contact about how Maria Santos tried to buy a five-hundred-thousand-dollar commission by seducing a prince." He smiled thinly. "They'll lap it up."

* * * * *

*What will it take for this billionaire prince to
realize he's falling in love with his mistress…?*
Look for
BILLIONAIRE PRINCE, PREGNANT MISTRESS
by Sandra Marton
Available July 2009
from Harlequin Presents®.

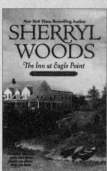
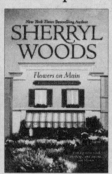
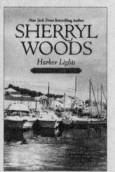

THE BELLES OF TEXAS

They're as strong as the state that raised them. The Belle sisters aren't afraid to go after what they want, whether it's reclaiming their ranch or their family.

Linda Warren
CAITLYN'S PRIZE

Thanks to her deceased father's gambling debts, Caitlyn Belle's beloved High Five Ranch is in dire straits. Particularly because the will stipulates that if the ranch doesn't turn a profit in six months, it must be sold to Judd Calhoun—the man Caitlyn jilted fourteen years ago. And Cait knows Judd has been waiting a long time for his revenge....

*Look for the first book
in The Belles of Texas miniseries,
on sale in July wherever books are sold.*

You're invited to join our Tell Harlequin Reader Panel!

By joining our new reader panel you will:

- Receive Harlequin® books—they are FREE and yours to keep with no obligation to purchase anything!
- Participate in fun online surveys
- Exchange opinions and ideas with women just like you
- Have a say in our new book ideas and help us publish the best in women's fiction

In addition, you will have a chance to win great prizes and receive special gifts! See Web site for details. Some conditions apply. Space is limited.

To join, visit us at
www.TellHarlequin.com.

THBPA0108

REQUEST YOUR FREE BOOKS!

2 FREE NOVELS PLUS 2 FREE GIFTS!

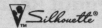

SPECIAL EDITION®

Life, Love and Family!

YES! Please send me 2 FREE Silhouette Special Edition® novels and my 2 FREE gifts (gifts are worth about $10). After receiving them, if I don't wish to receive any more books, I can return the shipping statement marked "cancel." If I don't cancel, I will receive 6 brand-new novels every month and be billed just $4.24 per book in the U.S. or $4.99 per book in Canada. That's a savings of at least 15% off the cover price! It's quite a bargain! Shipping and handling is just 50¢ per book.* I understand that accepting the 2 free books and gifts places me under no obligation to buy anything. I can always return a shipment and cancel at any time. Even if I never buy another book from Silhouette, the two free books and gifts are mine to keep forever.

235 SDN EYN4 335 SDN EYPG

Name _____ (PLEASE PRINT) _____

Address _____ Apt. # _____

City _____ State/Prov. _____ Zip/Postal Code _____

Signature (if under 18, a parent or guardian must sign)

Mail to the Silhouette Reader Service:
IN U.S.A.: P.O. Box 1867, Buffalo, NY 14240-1867
IN CANADA: P.O. Box 609, Fort Erie, Ontario L2A 5X3

Not valid to current subscribers of Silhouette Special Edition books.

Want to try two free books from another line?
Call 1-800-873-8635 or visit www.morefreebooks.com.

* Terms and prices subject to change without notice. Prices do not include applicable taxes. Sales tax applicable in N.Y. Canadian residents will be charged applicable provincial taxes and GST. Offer not valid in Quebec. This offer is limited to one order per household. All orders subject to approval. Credit or debit balances in a customer's account(s) may be offset by any other outstanding balance owed by or to the customer. Please allow 4 to 6 weeks for delivery. Offer available while quantities last.

Your Privacy: Silhouette is committed to protecting your privacy. Our Privacy Policy is available online at www.eHarlequin.com or upon request from the Reader Service. From time to time we make our lists of customers available to reputable third parties who may have a product or service of interest to you. If you would prefer we not share your name and address, please check here. ☐

SSE09R

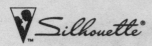
Silhouette®

COMING NEXT MONTH

Available June 30, 2009

#1981 THE TEXAS BILLIONAIRE'S BRIDE—Crystal Green
The Foleys and the McCords
For Vegas showgirl turned nanny Melanie Grandy, caring for the daughter of gruff billionaire Zane Foley was the perfect gig…until she fell for him, and her secret past threatened to bring down the curtain on her newfound happiness.

#1982 THE DOCTOR'S SECRET BABY—Teresa Southwick
Men of Mercy Medical
It was no secret that Emily Summers had shared a night of passion with commitment-phobe Dr. Cal Westen. But she kept him in the dark when she had their child. Would a crisis bring them together as a family…for good?

#1983 THE 39-YEAR-OLD VIRGIN—Marie Ferrarella
It wasn't easy when Claire Santaniello had to leave the convent to teach and take care of her sick mother. Luckily, widowed father and vice detective Caleb McClain was there for her as she found her way in the world…and into his arms.

#1984 HIS BROTHER'S BRIDE-TO-BE—Patricia Kay
Jill Jordan Emerson was engaged to a wealthy businessman several years her senior—until she came face-to-face with his younger brother Stephen Wells, a.k.a. the long-lost father of her son! Now which brother would claim this bride-to-be as his own?

#1985 LONE STAR DADDY—Stella Bagwell
Men of the West
It was a simple case of illegal cattle trafficking on a New Mexico ranch, and Ranger Jonas Redman thought he had the assignment under control—until the ranch's very single, very pregnant heiress Alexa Cantrell captured his attention and wouldn't let go….

#1986 YOUR RANCH OR MINE?—Cindy Kirk
Meet Me in Montana
When designer Anna Anderssen came home to Sweet River, she should have known she'd run right into neighboring rancher Mitchell Donovan, the one man who could expose the secrets—and reignite passions—that made her run in the first place!